Abe

Wonderful to meet

yo again :)

Hugs

dead man talking

a novel about life, death and love

ian lawton

RSP

First published in 2011 by Rational Spirituality Press.

All enquiries to be directed to www.rspress.org.

A CIP catalogue record for this title is available from the British
Library.

ISBN 978-0-9549176-9-2

Cover design by Ian Lawton.
Author photograph by Gaia Giakali.

PART ONE

one

I let the Black Beauty have its head. It was a turbocharged Porsche I'd kept for my own personal use for over a year – I didn't normally hold onto stock for that long, but this car was something special. And we sure needed some exhilaration for a change. We needed to feel... alive. I glanced across at her smiling face. She loved me driving fast, trusted me implicitly, knew that I wouldn't do anything silly even after a couple of drinks.

The twisting stretch of quiet country road that I knew like the back of my hand was a shortcut to our favourite club in the nearby town. It was a great test of man and machine, so good I often took customers along it to let them see what the object of their burning desire could do. And me and Beauty had mastered it together loads of times..

After a whole series of turns the road opened into a short straight, with a humpback bridge over a railway at the end. Accelerate hard through the lower gears, just touch eighty-five as he takes off, wait for him to land then a quick, hard dab on the brakes to steady him up before throwing him into a fast right hander. But still leave a margin for error. This is a road not a bloody race track, and the blind bend is lined on both sides with dense hedgerow interspersed with trees, with no verge or run-off.

Fantastic! As we hit the bridge there were no lights coming the other way, so I'd be able to use some of the other side of the road to straighten out the bend. Out of the corner of my eye I had a fleeting view of her throwing her head back and laughing as we flew through the air. Perfect landing, perfect turn-in, perfect apex and then...

dead man talking

Jeeeeeesus! In the headlights I caught the briefest of glimpses of an old farm truck, unlit, parked up on our side of the road – on the exact bit of tarmac we desperately needed. Instinctively I lifted off and slammed on the brakes, but the back end snapped round so viciously it would've been useless trying to steer into the slide, even if there had been enough time, which there wasn't, although that didn't stop the couple of seconds we were out of control and heading sideways straight for the back of the truck from feeling like a slow-motion eternity...

BANG!!

Then a deathly silence. It was all over in a flash.

two

So, here I am then. I know I'm going to die soon, but I'm not scared. Well, not really anyway. Of course I've got a few butterflies, but actually I'm quite looking forward to it. Anything to get away from this body, it's bloody useless and I've had enough of it. And, after all, I've already got some idea of where I'm going.

Sorry, I'm jumping ahead a bit. The name is Michael, Michael Prior. I'm a pretty down-to-earth sort of bloke, or at least I was until *it* happened. The crash that is. Most people call it an *accident*, but not me. But there I go again, jumping ahead.

Of course you want to know something about me, but if I'm honest there's not that much to tell. Like so many others I used to have an over-inflated opinion of myself, to think my life was pretty interesting, perhaps even that it would make a good book if anyone ever wanted to write it. But now I can see that most of it was very average, very run of the mill, that I was just another poor boy made good, fuelled by a gritty determination to better my station in life. Don't misunderstand me, there's nothing wrong with that, in fact there's a lot to be learnt from fighting your way up from humble beginnings by sheer hard graft. But it's all a question of balance. I know that now.

You know when people talk about having a mid-life crisis, when you question everything? I guess I've been having something like that ever since the crash, big time. After all, I lost my wife, didn't I? And there's nothing more guaranteed to shatter you, to make you feel like you've been slammed into a brick wall and left hopelessly trying to pick up the pieces, than the loss of your perfect lover and best friend all rolled into one.

4

dead man talking

I say mid-life crisis, but I'm only forty now and I was always in pretty good shape up until the crash. Not bad looking either, even if I say so myself. Not conventionally handsome perhaps, but certainly attractive enough that I had my fair share of conquests. But for all that they used to call me the lovable-rogue type before I met her, I loved Sinead with all my heart. I never looked at another woman after that, even though the offers didn't dry up.

Anyway, back to my crisis. Perhaps you think I've been trying to replace her since her death, seeing if I can still cut it with the girls? Don't be ridiculous! That's been the *last* thing on my mind, how on earth could I replace *her?* And even if I'd wanted to try, who'd have wanted *me* anyway, in this state?

Of course you do see plenty of rich, middle-aged poseurs with their young trophies hanging off their arms, and I've still got enough of the folding stuff that there'd have been plenty of fit young things only too desperate to get their hands on it, whatever the cost to their dignity. A lot of people live in a very, very material world – me included for most of my life – which is all kind of sad. But the way things are going, with whole working-class industries going to the wall while the bloody bankers and insurers and other moneymen are coining it, I can't see it changing any time soon. Ok, ok, I'll put the soapbox away. The point is that kind of girl didn't interest me before and doesn't interest me now. As for my Sinead, she was with me for me, screw the money. I know that. I *know* that.

And me? Well, as corny as it sounds, I knew I was supposed to be with her the moment I saw her. It was that sort of feeling you get right deep in your gut, when someone takes all your attention and then some. When, at least for a time, *no one* and *nothing else* matters.

dead man talking

Admittedly she was stunningly beautiful, and it wasn't only me that thought so because she had plenty of offers too. But I'd like to think I'd have married her even if she'd been as plain as the clothes she used to wear. She never did like fancy gear, my Sinead. Not like me. Flash bugger I was. The haircuts, the suits, all the trimmings. Not now though.

So no, my crisis hasn't been about women or girls, or even a more general image thing. You know how some blokes finally get hold of the flashy sports car or bike they could never afford when they were younger, and take to wearing what they think are trendy clothes? And then don't understand why most people laugh at them? Well it's not that either. You see I've had all that anyway, especially the expensive cars. They were my business, I *sold* them, and the very best ones at that. People used to come from all over to buy from me. Ferraris, Porsches, Mercedes, Maseratis, Lamborghinis. You name it, I could get it.

But that's all in the past now. I couldn't drive one of my cars any more even if I wanted to, which I don't. Because none of it matters. The cars, the money, the *things* – none of them *ever* mattered. I know that now. Just an endless stream of *stuff* that doesn't mean *shit*.

It's all changed. *I've* changed. I'm even past caring that my looks have gone. The last time I peered into a mirror I was confronted by a horror show. Not with the brilliant blue eyes that everyone used to admire, the blemish-free, tanned, taut skin and the shoulder-length blond hair. But with hollow eyes, thinning, greying hair and skin that looked like one of the hard-worked chamois leathers we used for cleaning the cars. All that perching precariously on top of a horrible, useless, motionless shell. Perhaps now you can understand why all I care about is finding Sinead again, and getting some proper answers.

Make no mistake, I want out. I'm off on a new journey. I don't know exactly where I'm going, but I know I'm going *somewhere*. Because my crisis wasn't prompted solely by losing my wife and the use of my body, as God-awful as that's been. It was prompted even more by what happened to me *during* the crash.

You see, I've already *seen* the other side.

three

As with any couple who are hopelessly in love, the day Sinead and I got married was the best of our lives – well, up to that point at least. We met at just the right time for both of us.

Born just as war ended, I was raised in a pretty tough, working-class area of south London. Money was always tight, although mum was a heroine making sure we didn't go hungry, and there was plenty of love too – especially because I was an only child. I think she had complications when she had me so couldn't have any more, but people didn't talk openly about things like that in those days. Anyway the whole of our street was like one big family, with everyone looking out for everyone else, and no one ever dreamed of locking their doors – not that any of us had anything worth nicking anyway. But from an early age we were taught to fight our own battles without relying on anyone else. We also learned to appreciate what little we had.

I wasn't very bright at school, although in truth I didn't really try very hard because learning by rote out of books never seemed to suit me. So I went out to work at the earliest opportunity, not least because we needed the money, when a friend of the family managed to get me an apprenticeship as a mechanic for a backstreet garage. To start with I was a real dogsbody, fetching and carrying, making cups of tea, cleaning up and so on. There was plenty of ribbing too but it was all good natured, and I picked things up pretty fast. I was lucky, I seemed to have a bit of a mechanical bent that I must have inherited from the Old Man.

Ahh, the Old Man. He served an apprenticeship as an

engineer with a big aircraft manufacturer during the war, after which he worked in a local machine shop. He was a real expert on a lathe, he had a large and a small one in the shed at home and could make anything with them – especially replacement parts for his beloved 1920s Rudge motorbike, which was immaculate but spares were getting harder and harder to source. As a boy I used to watch him for hours, spellbound as bland lumps of metal gradually took on the most amazing and intricate shapes of pistons, crankshafts, flywheels and so on. He was a real craftsman, taking real care over his work. Yet despite his obvious skill he seemed quite content to remain at the bottom of the ladder at work, never seeming to bring home much money.

In fact as far as I knew the amount of time he spent out in the shed was the only thing my parents ever disagreed about, although you wouldn't go as far as to call them arguments. That and the rare treats when he made me don an old helmet that was far too big and took me out to ride pillion. The bike was so noisy we could never do it without mum knowing, even if we pushed it right to the end of the narrow, grassy lane behind the shed before he started it. But even then I fancied that, for all her motherly concern over our safety, there was a hint of a smile at the corners of her mouth. And every now and then she even let him take *her* out for the day on it, right into the countryside, and they always seemed to be in a good mood when they got back.

In any case it wasn't long after I started work that I began to buy old-banger cars myself and fix them up in the street outside our house in my spare time. I made some half-decent money selling them on too, and over the next few years that built up until the Old Man was encouraging me to set up on my own. It seemed that what he lacked in ambition for himself he projected onto me.

I didn't mind, in fact I was flattered that he believed in me, but at first I wasn't convinced. I'd managed to put a bit of money aside but it wasn't enough to take the plunge and lose my weekly wage. Not when I added up all the costs of renting even a small workshop, what with the deposit and bills and everything, and of getting hold of some decent tools and equipment if I was going to do the job properly.

That's when he really surprised me one night as we sat up late, just chatting. During a lull, as we both stared into the fire, he put his hand inside his old tweed jacket and passed over a brown envelope that I could immediately tell was stuffed with notes.

"By the way, this is for you son." He tried to sound casual, as if he did this sort of thing every day.

"Where the hell did you get this Dad?" Without counting it, I could see from the wad of used fivers and tenners it was a tidy sum.

"I've sold the bike." His mouth curved slightly into the faintest smile, and there was a wonderful, loving sparkle in his eyes that I'd seen only a few times before. But that only made the situation all the more confusing. Surely he should've been at least a *bit* sad?

"What on earth have you done that for, that was your pride and bloody joy?" We weren't one of those working-class families that stood on ceremony.

"Because you need the money more than me son. It's for your future, and I know it will be far better than this." He cast his eyes around the small, homely but shabby room, and as I opened my mouth to protest again he stood up to cut me short. "You're taking it, and that's an end to it."

dead man talking

With that he bent over, kissed me on the forehead for what seemed just a little longer than usual, and went off to bed.

Three days later the stupid old bastard went and died on us. Actually he wasn't even old, only in his late forties. Sudden heart attack, out in the shed, the doctor said it would've been quick. I guess he must have known his time was limited. Of course poor mum was distraught, so I had to try to be strong for her, but by God I *missed* him. I still do. He wasn't just my dad he was my best friend too. In those last few years we used to talk for hours into the night, about everything. We didn't always agree but he still taught me how to be a man, how to treat others in my business and personal life, how to believe in myself – and how to value integrity above all else. And then he'd topped it all off by selling his most treasured possession and giving me the money.

So there I was, aged eighteen, with my own workshop. Over the next few years I repaired and sold more and more cars, always reinvesting in more expensive stock. The sixties were beginning to swing but I didn't take much notice, I was putting in very long hours. I was determined to make it work, for him just as much as for me.

And it paid off. Several times I expanded into better local premises, gradually taking on a few other mechanics and a salesman, until by the start of the seventies I'd moved the business south to an imposing showroom in the heart of the Home Counties. This was where the serious money was, and it was the ideal environment for me to fulfil my ambitions and start selling the real exotica. I was relatively young, still only in my mid-twenties, but I worked hard and knew my stuff and somehow older people never seemed to question my age. I didn't even need to get my own hands dirty any more, not unless I wanted to, or if there was a problem no one else could fix. I made so much money in those first few years after the move that I was able to buy an equally imposing country house nearby.

I'd been in my new home for nearly two years before I met her. There I was, nicely set up but rattling around in a house that was far too big for just one person. I'd asked mum to move down to help me fill out the space, but she was set in her ways and didn't want to leave the life she knew and the friends she loved. Nor did she want to leave the house she'd shared with the Old Man, God bless her. Of course I made sure she no longer had to worry about money, and I tried to get up to visit her when I could. But not as often as I should have and, truth be told, it tended to be only if I was going that way to look at a car.

In the absence of any close family around me, and I guess to make up for the youth I'd missed out on by working so hard, I threw lavish parties most Saturday nights. They became pretty well known, there were lots of hangers on and it usually got pretty debauched and out of hand. But after a while I knew I wanted something more, especially as my thirtieth birthday started to loom on the horizon. I had lots of girlfriends – who wouldn't in my position? – but nothing too serious, on my side at least. And that's when she walked into the showroom, one glorious, sunny Saturday afternoon.

She was so very beautiful. Not especially tall, but her simple, yellow, summer dress was tight enough to reveal a figure to die for. Her long auburn hair tumbled down over her shoulders, framing *such* a face: hardly any make up; huge, innocent brown eyes; a long, thin, distinguished nose; naturally red lips; and a complexion of pure porcelain. She carried herself with that quietly self-confident air that all people born into real, old money have. As if all that wasn't enough, when she spoke her gorgeous, dusky voice carried a soft Irish lilt. And from that moment on I was gone, spellbound, gobsmacked... totally, hopelessly and irretrievably lost.

I guess it's a horrible thing to say but she made most of the other girls I'd known seem like vulgar tarts on the make. I wanted to cradle her face in my hands there and then, to kiss that beautiful mouth long and hard. But I knew I couldn't just jump in there as I normally would, all patter and charm. That wouldn't work with this one, I needed to be more subtle. More... natural, actually.

Luckily she was in a terrific mood and had celebration in mind. About five years younger than me, she'd been training as a nurse for several years – clearly the fact that her family had money didn't mean she was idle. And she'd only ever had old bangers for cars, so she'd promised herself a sporty little convertible if she passed her exams, which she had that very day. She'd spotted the little red MGB nestling in the corner of the showroom a few weeks before, so now she was here, determined that she'd be driving it away. "You'll be leaving with a whole lot more than you bargained for," I said to myself.

Funnily enough this little car wasn't the sort I'd normally get involved with. Admittedly it was low mileage and immaculate, but it was small and relatively cheap, and normally if cars like that came in as part exchanges I'd ship them straight out to another dealer. But I'd gone to an auction and been outbid on a couple of cars, and then there it was and for some reason I liked the look of it. I hadn't inspected it properly beforehand, so I put in a few half-hearted bids and all of a sudden my rivals pulled out far earlier than I expected. So the little gem was mine for a pretty low price. The rest of the team nearly wet themselves when I came back with it, all six-feet-two of me crammed into the tiny cockpit, trying to lever myself out backwards until my upper half was spread-eagled on the floor while I tried to wriggle my legs free.

Afterwards, whenever Sinead talked about how we met, she'd stress that unusual things like that always happen when two people are supposed to be together. She seemed to be implying that it was all somehow planned in advance, but I never really understood what she meant. All I cared about was that the little red car had brought her to me, and that was good enough.

So I know it's something of a cliché, but for us it really was love at first sight. During a wonderful dinner that night we both felt like we'd known each other for years, and everything flowed so freely that, when I got down on bended knee and proposed, I'd never been more sure about anything in my whole life. She didn't scream out, that wasn't her way, but she gave me the biggest smile ever and jumped into my arms, knocking us both onto the floor where we kissed passionately in front of all the other diners – which was poor form really, especially for a girl with her upbringing, but to be honest we just didn't care.

Finally she pulled her mouth away and, rolling on top of me and pinning my arms above my head, she locked her piercing gaze onto mine. "Yes my love, I will." Which was lucky, because I'd dashed out that afternoon to buy a ring as soon as she left the showroom, and it had cost me a *lot* more than her car.

I booked the flights the next day, and four weeks later we were flying to Cancun to get married on the beach.

four

No one minded that we got married alone with just a couple we met over there as witnesses, especially given that I organised a *very* extravagant piss up for everyone who'd have been invited when we got back. – marquee on the lawn, top band, crate loads of champagne, the works.

But first off let me tell you, those two weeks in Mexico were pure ecstasy. Despite our different backgrounds we had so much in common, like the same taste in films and music, although Sinead read far more widely than I did and had far more general knowledge. It wasn't that I was stupid, far from it, but all I'd ever really cared about was cars and making money from them. I'd had little time to develop other interests.

The only major difference between us was something I never really grasped until it was too late – her underlying sense of what I guess you might call the *spiritual*. She didn't talk about it much, or at least not in an obvious way – not like her mother. And it wasn't like she was religious, even though her father was a devout Catholic and she'd attended a posh Dublin convent. Apparently various priests and mother superiors had tried so hard to shove the Blessed Virgin down her throat from an early age that when she left Ireland she rebelled, but she liked to say that she hadn't thrown the baby out with the bathwater.

My parents were staunch Church of England, and God was certainly called upon in our house on a regular basis, although we didn't go to church except on special occasions. But as I'd grown older I'd found it harder and harder to take the whole thing seriously. After all, as far as I could tell people only really prayed when they were right in the shit, while if they did it any other time, say in church, it seemed they were merely repeating old-fashioned words by rote that meant bugger all to them, just because they were supposed to.

My aunty Mary didn't help. She'd married an estate agent and they lived in one of the better suburbs out west. She seemed to think she was much better than us, she was always talking in her fake-posh voice about how God looked after her and was merciful and so on and so forth, and scolding my mum and dad for not going to church more often – *they* went every Sunday, lah di dah. But she was one of the most unkind, unloving, inconsiderate people I ever met. Even when she helped out part-time in a charity shop it seems it was only so she could boast about it.

So I'd decided fairly early on that this whole God malarkey wasn't for me, that you didn't need it to be a decent person. And that when the going got tough you needed to rely on *yourself* and your *own* inner strength, and shouldn't suddenly expect some all-powerful superbeing to be there to bail you out.

I now know I was right and wrong all at the same time. But until the crash I was a go-getter, the world was my oyster and I had little time for superstitious nonsense. By contrast Sinead had this deep serenity that came from some kind of more general spiritual belief. I never really knew exactly what it was because, if I'm honest, I used to switch off if she ever tried to talk about it. It wasn't that I didn't admire the way she was, and I know there was an inner part of me even then that wanted to listen. But I guess there was another part that wanted to push it all away, pretend it didn't exist, and focus on the things that *really* mattered – the work and the money and the cars and the houses and all the rest. As you already know, *that* was *then*.

That gap in our communication aside there was really nothing to spoil our happiness. I worked hard but Sinead didn't seem to mind, and she continued to work herself even though she didn't need to. And I was ok with that, I liked her independence, I was never one of those men who expected to have their little wifey waiting at home, gin and tonic at the ready and the dinner warm on the table. Plus we had a pretty lively social life, and all the beach and skiing holidays we could want, so it was all pretty good. Wonderful, in fact.

But as our early years together flew by and Sinead moved towards her late twenties, the more the talk turned to us starting a family. I must admit I'd never been unduly bothered about having children – I guess being so wrapped up in my work I was basically a pretty selfish bloke. But the more I thought about it the more I warmed to the idea, while Sinead's body clock was obviously becoming increasingly insistent. So when she told me she'd taken her last pill for a while, I was just as excited as she was.

It didn't take long. The Old Man always said the men in our family line produced good little swimmers, and Sinead was obviously from good stock too. She flew through the pregnancy and birth with few complications. And when I held little Zak for the first time, and looked deep into his eyes, I experienced a depth of emotion I'd never have thought possible. I wouldn't say it was more than what I felt for Sinead, it was just different. The sense of love mingled with responsibility was beyond words.

Unfortunately this blissful state wasn't to last. Initially Zak seemed to be a happy and contented baby, but after only a few months he started to cry almost non-stop. Neither of us could work out what the problem was, and a series of tests by our doctor and at the hospital revealed nothing out of the ordinary. We were all at a loss.

The stress of Zak's constant crying put far more pressure on Sinead than me. She'd given up work several months before he was born, and now here she was marooned at home with a baby who, however much we loved him, wasn't exactly a barrel of laughs. At least I could get away to work during the day. I pleaded with her to let me employ a nanny to take some of the strain, but she was adamant that Zak was *her* son and needed *her*, not some stranger.

That wasn't all. While she was pregnant we'd had a few chats about how we wanted to bring him up, although they didn't amount to much. But once he was born I was keen to get a place reserved at a top-flight private school. Sinead didn't agree, and one night we had our first – and as it turned out only – real argument. It was foul.

"Look, I've worked bloody hard to get where I am today, and I want him to have all the chances I can give him that me and my dad never had."

"But there are perfectly good state schools we could send him to. Why do you think you can *buy* everything? What about all the children whose parents can't afford private schooling?"

"I don't give a shit about them. This is us, and we *can* afford it, and I want to give him the best."

"Why the hell do you think money and privilege are going to be what's best for him? What's he going to learn from that? To *shit* on people just like you?"

"That's a bloody awful thing to say! I never deliberately shit on anyone!"

"Ah but you don't mind screwing people into the ground to make the most money you can on your *deals*."

"But that's *business*, for Christ's sake! That's how it's done, or didn't you know? How the hell do you think we can afford to live in this place?"

"I wouldn't give a toss if we lived in a hole in the ground as long as we could sleep soundly at night, with no guilt."

"I've got nothing to feel guilty about and I sleep fine, thanks very much, or at least I did until that little bleeder was bo..." It had all got too much for me at last, but as soon as the words were out of my mouth I regretted them like I'd never regretted anything before.

"You... you bastard." Her words tailed off and she started to sob violently. I reached over and grabbed her to me, holding her close. At first she was stiff with anger.

"I'm so sorry love... so, so sorry. I didn't mean that. It was just... just the heat of the moment." By now I too was fighting to hold back the tears as she softened against my chest.

"I know, I know. We're both under pressure. And I guess it's my own guilt about my expensive schooling coming out too, coupled with a generous helping of good old Catholic guilt just for good measure. It sticks like glue you know, you think you've got it licked then out it pops again when you least expect it." She looked up at me and smiled weakly, but then her tear-stained face took on an earnest look. "But seriously sweetheart, can't you see that all this, this house, our holidays, our cars, even most of our friends... it's all so *false*. I don't want Zak to grow up thinking this is what it's all about. I sometimes think he'd be better off if we didn't have any money at all."

"So what's brought all this on love?"

"I've always felt like this. It's just you've never bothered to listen."

But I still didn't get it. I didn't get it at all. And that night I had the most terrifying nightmare. Sinead was standing with her hand on some sort of gate, looking back at me as she prepared to walk through it. And I got the overwhelming sense that I couldn't follow her.

That somehow she was leaving me.

five

New England, 1693

As one of the most respected tradesmen in the small community, and a staunch pillar of the Church, Saul Bellows was in no mood to listen to his wife's protestations.

"But husband, these women are innocent. The charges laid at their door are false. They are good, God-fearing women, and they used to be our friends. How can you now think this of them?"

"What nonsense is this, woman? They have sold their souls to Satan himself, and they must pay the price! You have seen what has happened to the children, with their wailing and fitting. One of them even threw the Good Book at her father. The Good Book itself! These children have been bewitched woman, and we all know these two women are responsible."

"Saul, you are my husband, you are a good and righteous man, and I have promised to love and obey you come what may. But I cannot go against God's will. I believe these women are innocent, and I cannot stand by and see them hanged. If you will not support me, I will do it myself, alone. I must speak up for them when they are brought to trial."

six

It doesn't matter how much in love you are, if you want to stay that way you need to keep the fire burning, to feed it with fuel. So Sinead and I had always agreed that we'd try to get out together once a fortnight, or once a month at worst, just the two of us – to a cinema, restaurant, pub, whatever.

We were intent on sticking to this plan after Zak was born too, but it went out the window as soon as his problems started. She simply didn't feel up to it, and remained adamant that she didn't want to leave him with anyone else. Every now and then she'd suggest I go out for a drink without her, perhaps with a few mates, but I didn't want to leave her to cope alone in the evenings as well. Yet her thirtieth birthday was fast approaching and, although it was pretty obvious any sort of surprise party would go down like a lead balloon, we planned – well I planned, because Sinead still couldn't muster any great enthusiasm – a little celebration for just the two of us. She'd been housebound with the little fellow for quite a few months and I felt more than ever that a decent night out – a nice meal, perhaps a dance and a drink at a club afterwards – would really help to ease the strain, would be something for us both to look forward to.

When the great day arrived Zak was still up and down and the one babysitter she had some confidence in, her mother, had had a heavy cold for several days. Sinead was doubtful and it looked like we might have to call things off. But at the eleventh hour her mother stubbornly insisted, in spite of Sinead's protestations, that she was much better, that we needed a night out, and that she'd look after him as agreed.

dead man talking

Ah, the lovely Jocasta. You haven't met her yet, have you? Of course that isn't her real name. She was born plain little Brenda Murphy, in the suburbs of Dublin, but not long out of her teens she used her looks and Irish charm to marry into a wealthy dynasty. Sinead was born soon after, and life went along reasonably until Brenda discovered the hippy movement in the mid sixties. Within a few years her rebellious side just couldn't be silenced any more and she left her husband – apparently he was an old tyrant anyway – to embark on a new life across the water. She was in her late thirties and Sinead, now in her late teens, agreed she too was ready for a new challenge.

That's also when Brenda changed her name to Jocasta, just for good measure, and ever since she'd been hanging out with her hippy pals, all tie-dyes and multi-coloured kaftans and whatnot. There was even some suspicion she'd gone the whole nine yards and was now batting for the other team, or at least didn't really care whose side she was on. But Sinead didn't seem to mind, and I certainly didn't begrudge her a bit of variety if that's what she wanted.

More than anything I was grateful she'd passed her stunning looks on to her daughter. Even though by now she'd just turned fifty you could easily see why she'd been able to marry so far above her station, and the two of them were still regularly mistaken for sisters. They both had milky white skin but Jocasta's long, flame-red hair formed even more of a contrast. And they both had terrific figures, although Jocasta was somewhat larger in the chest area – not that that particularly appealed to me except visually, I was always more of a nipples man anyway and, on that score, I had no complaints about my wonderful wife.

dead man talking

Looks aside, underneath it all our mutual working-class background formed a certain bond between Jocasta and me. But, whereas I was proud of mine, she made every effort to cover hers up. The airs and graces she put on used to really grate on me. But the worst bit was her continual banging on about bloody star signs – not to mention her past lives, and the karma she was getting rid of, and how she was such an old soul, and this was definitely her last time on earth, and all the rest of that old bollocks. Well, it certainly sounded like bollocks then, and much of it still does now. Sinead didn't seem to have much time for a lot of it either, but she took it more in her stride and was still close to her mother. I just used to walk out the room.

Anyway, when Jocasta arrived that night to look after Zak he seemed to calm down a little, and Sinead did too. She went upstairs to get dressed and, for the first time since he was born, made a real effort. She didn't need to do it for me – I always thought she was beautiful at any time of day or night, and whatever she was or wasn't wearing – but she clearly needed to do it for herself. Jocasta had *insisted* that she make a grand entrance by gliding down the staircase into the hall, and the change was astonishing. She had that carefree radiance again and I had to work hard to hold back the tears. This is the picture of her etched into my memory: hair piled up in a pleat; plain, knee-length, red-satin dress hugging her still remarkably slim body; the coy and knowing smile... I've got to stop now. I'm afraid that memory still proves too much for me, even after all these years.

After Sinead had checked for the umpteenth time that Jocasta had the number of the restaurant – hardly bloody necessary given that she had lunch there most days – she held Zak in her arms. He was still and calm

dead man talking

now, a rare event, and they gazed into each other's eyes for what seemed an eternity. She slowly handed him to her mother then, as she was about to follow me through the front door, turned back and looked lovingly at him, then her mother, and finally at me. I thought I detected a certain sadness in her eyes, but I put it down to her worrying about leaving her baby for the first time in months. Ever since I've replayed that scene again and again, wondering if she knew something was about to happen. After what happened with the Old Man perhaps I should've guessed, but I didn't.

We started the evening with a quick drink at our local, the White Hart. Centuries old and traditional, it's ambience was completed by Sean, the affable and highly successful owner who was also a good friend. It was a place we both loved although we hadn't been there together for months, and we were warmly received at the bar. But this was no time for banter with Sean or the locals, they'd all heard about our problems with Zak and they understood. I carried our drinks over to a quiet table in the corner and it was wonderful to be out, just the two of us together. It felt almost as if we were courting all over again.

Then it was on to the restaurant nearby – another beautiful old thatched place, terrific chef, expensive but worth every penny – where I'd booked our favourite table in the alcove at the back. I was a pretty valued customer because I lunched there regularly with clients, so the food, wine and service were superb as always. Time flew by. We talked, laughed, even cried a little when we discussed Zak and what the hell might be wrong with him. But we didn't dwell on that. Intuitively neither of us wanted to spoil this precious time together.

We'd had an aperitif in the pub, then shared a bottle of

wine with the meal, so Sinead was getting pretty merry – I felt fine, but she was somewhat out of practice.

"You want to go home now, darling? It's your birthday, your call." I was puffing away on a large Cuban, small glass of port in the other hand, vintage of course. She'd already called home, and Jocasta had reassured her that Zak had gone off easily for once and was sleeping soundly. Still I didn't want to push her – but then I'd temporarily forgotten that tonight I was with the old Sinead again.

"No way! Come on, let's go dancing, let our hair down. I want to finish this night with a bang!" She removed the clips from her hair, and shook it free. I know I keep saying it but my God she was beautiful.

She probably didn't need steadying, but I wrapped my arm round her shoulder as we walked out anyway, just to be sure – the waiters' flirtatious "wonderful to see you again, Mrs. Prior"... "you look so radiant tonight, Mrs. Prior"... "please come and see us again soon, Mrs. Prior"... ringing in our ears. I was used to taking a back seat when Sinead was around, and I couldn't blame them for loving her almost as much as I did.

We jumped in and I let the Black Beauty have its head...

seven

What the *hell* is going on? I can see the wreckage of my car... my beautiful, expensive Black Beauty... wrapped, *literally* wrapped around the back of the truck... they've both been shoved a long way up the road... it all looks pretty bad... the passenger side's hardly there any more, it's been concertina'd right down into just a few inches.

On no, no, NO!!! That's where Sinead was... there's no way she can have survived that... I've fucking *killed* her!! NO NO NO NO NO!!!

Get a grip man, get a grip!! There may be some small chance... got to get help... call for the fire brigade to cut her out... and an ambulance... there's a house over there, light on... must get there fast, use their telephone.

Whooaa... what the hell just happened? Suddenly I'm right on the doorstep! Must have blacked out on the way over or something... anyway calm down man, ring the bell... come *on*, got to *hurry!*

Uh? I've just reached out to press the bell and my hand went straight through the bloody door frame!! This is getting stupid... I can't make the bell ring at all! Shit... better see what I can do myself... must get back and flag down another car.

Whoa... not again, how'd I get back here so *fast?* Hang on... what's that hanging out the smashed window on the driver's side? It looks like an arm, all covered in blood... oh shit... it's *my* arm! That's my Rolex on the wrist, with the face all smashed... this little lot is going to cost me a fortune... anyway, never mind about that now... come *on*, focus!

dead man talking

Wait a minute... what the *hell* am I doing up here? I've just realised I'm *floating!!* And how come I can look down at my arm and it's right here in front of me, and then I look over there at the wreckage and it's there as well? This doesn't make any sense.

Anyway... come *on*... still no cars passing... I need to get round the passenger side... help Sinead if I can. Wow! I only had to think about that and it happened... I really seem to be able to just fly anywhere I like... this could be fun! Wait, no... stop pissing about Michael, this is serious... can't see anything on this side... truck's in the way... better get back round the driver's side... and bing! here I am again... no climbing down or walking around.

Hey... now I can see my face inside... what a bloody *mess*. Yuk! But you know what? I don't seem to care much... how *weird*... I'm sure I *ought* to care... but I just can't be bothered somehow.

Slow down a minute Michael... this isn't making any sense... let's think it through... I'm here... I seem to have a body... I'm thinking just the same as I ever did... ok, maybe I feel a bit detached somehow, but I'm still *me*... and yet I can't be me... because *that's* me trapped in the car... isn't it? Oh no... no no no no no NO! I'm not... am I? Don't even ask yourself Michael... shut up, I've got to ask! I am, aren't I? I'm... *dead*.

Ok, come on now, calm down... this death thing doesn't seem so bad after all... look you can fly you fool, you've always wanted to do that... whoosh... this is *terrific*, I feel just like a kid again! And so light, so free! But wait, where the hell is Sinead? Is she dead too?

Hang on, is that her up there? So she must be then... why isn't she waiting for me? Sinead... SINEAD... wait for me love... hang on! Damn, she's getting away... I've got to try and catch her up.

We seem to be flying through some sort of tunnel in the sky... I'm getting a sense of speed, like stuff is whizzing past but there's nothing really there any more... it's all dark but there seems to be a light at the end... it's getting bigger and bigger... and brighter and brighter... nearing the end now.

My God, what *is* this place? It feels so peaceful... like I'm surrounded by... by what? What *is* this intense feeling? Whoa... fantastic... oh I'm loving this... this is better than making love to Sinead, and that's saying something... it's completely taking me over... hang on... it's *love*... pure *love! That's* what it is.

Wait... there's someone coming towards me... is it Sinead? She was up ahead somewhere... Dad? Dad!! It's you! Oh wow wow WOW!! You old bastard, I thought I was never going to see you again! This is fan-bloody-tastic... it feels like we're hugging... but it's better than that... almost like we're one person!

I could do this forever... but I've got to find Sinead... where *is* she? Over *there!* There's a kind of gate and she's going through it... I can't really see what's beyond... it just seems to be more of this shining *light* everywhere... I've got to go after her... Sinead, love, wait... *please* wait... let me catch up with you... let's go *together* like we always do! She's looking round at me now... oh God she looks *so* beautiful... but sad as well... why won't she let me catch up with her? All I want is to *hold* her... Sinead! Sinead!! *Please* slow down!

Oh no... no!! This is the scene I saw in my nightmare... the one when I wasn't allowed to follow her!

Dad... stop it... what are you doing? Let me *go*... I've got to go after Sinead! What the hell do you mean I've got to let her go? Look, leave me be will you! How come you can stop me from moving when you're not even touching me? What the *hell* are you doing? Look dad... you've got to let me *go*... if you don't I'm going to have to smack you one old son... I don't want to but... oh shit, I've just remembered... I can't do that here can I? *Please* dad, let me go won't you? Alright, alright, I'll try to calm down... but just let me go to her! What do you mean I'm not allowed to? Who bloody says? She's my wife and she *needs* me, and I need her! For pity's sake, *pleeease*... come on, look, she's *disappearing*... I'm in pieces here... I've never cried in front of you before, *never*... come *on*, this isn't fair!

Ok, ok, I feel your hug and your love... my God, look at me... weeping like a baby... yes, I *know* you want me to go back, but I'm sorry dad... this is hard... *bloody* hard... I just don't understand... I don't want to go back, not without Sinead... I can't do it on my own... either let me stay here with her, or let her come back with me!

Please don't make me go back on my own... I don't want to go back into that body... it was all broken up, I saw it... please! What do you mean I just have to, it will all become clear in the end? *How* will it? *Why can't you tell me?*

I guess you've worked out I was pretty reluctant to climb back into this body. I was sort of propelled back down the tunnel, and then I could see the wreckage and a police car and a fire engine and an ambulance and two men bent over the other me lying inside it, one pumping my chest while the other tried to breathe air into my lungs. But I was still resisting, fighting it.

"It's no use, he's gone and I'm knackered!" The one

pumping my chest straightened up wearily.

"No, no, we've *got* to keep trying!" insisted the other. "I know Mike Prior, we used to drink in the same local, he's a good bloke, fixed me up with a cheap car privately once. *It* never let *me* down, and *I'm* not going to let *him* down now." He began alternately pumping my chest and breathing into my mouth. I got closer and he was right, I recognised him from some years back. He was really putting some effort in. I just wished the bloody car I'd found for him had let him down.

Suddenly I felt some sort of jolt pulling me in and whoosh! I was back inside my body again. It felt cold, and heavy, and really, really bad.

"I've got him! He's back! HE'S BACK!!"

eight

By the time the trial commenced a whisper had been circulating that Martha Bellows sympathised with the accused women, but no one knew for sure. One by one the prosecution witnesses worked themselves into a frenzy of accusation, certain in the knowledge that their righteousness would earn them a place in heaven. Then, hesitantly, just as the Elders were about to deliver their verdict, she stood up to face the packed, riotous courtroom. Gradually the tumult died down until there was complete silence.

"You have something to say, Mistress Bellows?"

"I have, sir." She cast an anxious glance at her husband seated on the other side of the room. He did not return the compliment but stared straight ahead, expressionless.

"Pray continue then. But choose your words carefully mistress. I warn you this court is in no mood to hear yet more blasphemy." She looked around the rest of the room, longing to see some sign of support. There was none – only the cold, hard faces of angry people waiting for their chance to pounce. What had all these people, for so long her friends, become? The two accused stared at her pitifully, their abject terror briefly replaced by a glimmer of hope. She took one last, deep breath and steeled herself for what was surely to come.

"Good sirs, I am only a humble servant of the Lord, but I must protest at the treatment of these women. This court is a mockery, the evidence all fabrication and hearsay. These women you accuse have done *nothing* wrong. The children you say they have bewitched are suffering from nothing more than a natural, childish desire for attention. But, fuelled by our stupidity in taking their delusions seriously, their behaviour has become unruly and wicked. And instead of stamping it out we have been condoning and even encouraging it. The blame lies entirely with *us*. And *you*, sirs, have allowed a misplaced sense of religious duty to blind you so much you abuse your powers. What has become of the Lord's message of charity, forgiveness and love? I beg you to release these two innocent women and stop this nonsense."

Although Martha delivered this plea with increasing volume and pace, the bulk of her words were drowned out as the courtroom erupted with fury. Everywhere she looked she could see faces contorted with hatred, their snarling mouths spitting vicious abuse in her direction. Through the throng she caught a brief glimpse of her husband, the only person still seated and impassive, although he was now attracting his own share of bile. Surely he could not allow his wife to talk this way, unopposed? How could he so stunningly fail to control and correct her?

"She's one of them! One of them! Hang them all!!" Up went the cry from the back, and as one the surging mob picked up the chant. The Elders tried in vain to regain control, but they were powerless in the face of such anarchy as Martha and the other women were dragged from the courtroom, screaming in terror. In no time three ropes were being thrown over the branches of an enormous old oak on the edge of town.

Saul remained inside the courtroom alone. He appeared, at least on the outside, as impassive as ever. But the whites of his knuckles showed that he was clutching his hat very, very hard.

nine

So that's how my life was turned upside down. I was on life support for about a week, and remained in coma for several more. I had various operations to repair ruptured internal organs and so on, but the one thing they could do nothing about was my broken neck. I was paralysed from there down, and would remain that way for good.

And would you believe I was aware of much of this even while it was happening? It's a funny thing now I look back on it because everyone assumes, especially doctors and nurses, that when you're in coma there's nothing going on upstairs. And I'd have agreed with them. But that's so wrong! When the nurses used to say things like, "Look at that poor guy, he was so successful and now he's such a mess, I wonder if he'll even make it?" it used to really piss me off, because I knew I was going to pull through whether I wanted to or not.

Sometimes they'd say, "The poor man, he doesn't even know his wife's dead." That was a real cracker, that one. I was only too well aware that Sinead was gone for good, and my heart was *breaking*.

Not only that but I blamed myself so much the pain was almost unbearable. If only I'd had a bit less to drink, or hadn't been driving quite so fast! I'd killed her, as surely as if I'd put a knife through her heart. Fully sober I would've suppressed the instinct to lift off the throttle, because all decent drivers of rear-engined cars know that makes the back end snap round. And while I couldn't have risked aiming the car through the hedgerow at the edge of the road, not with all those trees, if I'd kept all four wheels in line I might just've been able to jink to the right of the truck at the last moment. We still might've struck it a

34

glancing blow, but we wouldn't have ended up wrapped right round the back of it. And my poor Sinead wouldn't have taken the brunt of the impact.

Anyway, even if it hadn't been my fault, what sort of justice would take away a beautiful, intelligent, kind-hearted girl like her, especially from her baby son, and let a useless, selfish oaf of a man like me live on? And to cap it all it wasn't even as if I was going to be able to look after Zak, the state I was in. So if you think my depression is deep now, you should've seen me *then*.

The only thing that made those first weeks at all bearable was when I found I could still *leave* my body, just by switching my focus away from it and thinking about where I wanted to be. I couldn't go back into the tunnel with the light at the end any more, it didn't seem to be around, but I could go wherever I liked in earthly terms. It was pretty much as before, I was aware of having a body of sorts, a kind of replica of my normal body except this one wasn't all beaten up. But this time I got used to the fact that it didn't behave like my normal body at all, that it didn't interact with objects or people. I could just pass through walls, doors and ceilings and, most of the time, no one even knew I was there. There were exceptions though, because every now and then people would look up or across at me and seem to sense my presence. But I was too wrapped up in myself to try to communicate with them.

Of course flying around the place was infinitely preferable to lying comatose on a hospital bed wired up to all sorts of apparatus, and any other time this would've been a fantastic opportunity. But wherever I went I couldn't shake off the excruciating anguish and guilt. All I could hope for was just to take my mind off things, to distract myself, even if only for a short while.

So I got around a bit but in my mental state I couldn't raise much enthusiasm for my new found powers. Most of the time I was just moping about, not even taking much notice of my surroundings. Except every now and then something would catch my attention, and jolt me out of my stupor.

One time I accidentally floated into the bedroom of a house I happened to be passing, not really thinking about where I was going, and saw a couple tenderly making love. It *ripped* me apart. Never again would I be able to hold Sinead like that. For an instant I was so jealous and distraught I thought about hurling something at them – I sensed that at that moment the intensity of my feelings *would've* allowed me to move something physical just with my thoughts. But then I realised how unfair that would be, and got out fast.

Another time I was passing a house and heard a couple having a furious row. I know it sounds terrible but I was attracted to that because I thought it would make me feel better, so I floated in for a ringside seat. And do you know what they were arguing about? A tin of peas. That's right! *A tin of bloody peas!* Apparently the wife had bought the wrong sort because the shop had run out of the ones her husband liked, and he was going absolutely berserk! Fair play to the woman, at least she was sticking up for herself and giving him a fair old caning back about some of his own shortcomings. But it wasn't long before I couldn't bear to listen any more. Some people only appreciate what they've got after they've lost it, whereas I'd loved Sinead with all my heart, but *still* she'd been taken from me.

No she hadn't. *I'd* taken her from me, and from everyone

else, with my own stupidity.

I guess you might think that while roaming around I'd have been drawn to our home, but at first I couldn't bear the thought of seeing Zak, not after what I'd done to his mother. In any case Jocasta would almost certainly have moved in and be doing a good job of looking after him, even though she too would be in pieces. And although he already had his problems, at least he was way too young to be aware of what I'd done.

Or so I thought, until finally I plucked up the courage to visit him.

ten

I was really scared about going to our home, but in the end I knew I *had* to do it. I spent some time trying to calm myself, then I focussed on the front door and I was there. Jocasta's car was in the drive as expected so I knew they were in. I hesitated, taking in the familiar surroundings. Somehow they didn't feel the same now.

Come on Michael, you can't delay this any longer. I floated through the door and hall, on into the living room, and there they were. Jocasta was quietly cradling her grandson in her arms, rocking him from side to side. She immediately seemed different somehow, more serene – more like Sinead, it struck me. As for poor Zak, he'd definitely grown in the few weeks since I'd seen him, he was turning into a fine looking little lad. But his crying appeared to be just as bad as ever.

Yet after I'd been there for a few moments, just staring at the two of them, he stopped crying and seemed to look round towards me. Then he closed his eyes and began to drift off to sleep. Obviously glad to take a break, Jocasta laid him down in his cot and walked towards the kitchen door. It was just him and me. I moved closer, emotions welling up.

"It's ok dad."

What the...?! As if my mind hadn't been turned upside down enough over recent weeks, here was my six-month-old son talking to me! But, just like the Old Man after the crash, his words – well, not so much words as *thoughts* – seemed to just float into my head, and I was able to respond with my own. The only difference was I couldn't see Zak floating in any sort of separate body, he was merely there in his cot with his eyes shut. Of course I couldn't pick him up or cuddle him as I so desperately wanted, but my thought response was automatic.

"I love you son, and I've missed you. How are you?"

"Oh, I'm ok. I know what happened dad, and I know about mum. I also know it wasn't your fault." This left me dumbstruck and I seemed to collapse inwards, unable to control my emotions at all. But gradually I composed myself.

"Son, look, this is terribly hard for me. I'd had a few drinks that night, and I was driving fast, and..."

"You hit a truck that shouldn't have been there, that you couldn't possibly have avoided under any circumstances. No one could." His thoughts felt so calm, so reassuring.

"Of course I could. I could've..." Hang on a minute. However mature my infant son appeared to be, I wasn't about to get into an exchange about the finer points of controlling a rear-engined car, so I deliberately blocked the stream of thought that was about to pour out. And anyway, forget about all that! Sure I should've been getting used to everything I'd known being turned upside down, but this was at least as crazy as anything else I'd experienced in recent weeks. Why the *hell* was I able to talk to him *at all?* And why did he have such clarity, and maturity of thought? Needless to say Zak picked up on my confusion.

"Us babies are a lot brighter than everyone thinks, dad. We don't forget everything about who we really are and where we've just come from all at once. By the time we start talking and running around we've lost a lot of it, even though we might still get flashbacks for a few years after that. But I'm still at that stage when I'm sleeping a lot, and that's when I'm not really in here – just like you're not in your body now – and can use my full awareness."

This was all a bit too much for me and I didn't fully understand what he was saying, but I didn't feel like pressing him. In any case now I had the opportunity there was something else I desperately wanted to ask. Again he answered before I'd had chance to formalise the thought.

"Why do I cry all the time?"

"Well, yes."

"Because my leg hurts! My left leg. *You* hurt it when you rolled over accidentally on top of me in bed one night!"

"Oh... oh, Zak, my baby. I'm so, so, sorry. We just didn't *know*."

"It's ok dad. Just get it fixed for me, will you, *please*? Now you'd better go because grandma's coming back."

"Why, will she be able to hear us, or tune in to whatever it is we're doing?"

"No, she's not that sensitive, even though she likes to *think* she is." We both chuckled. "Don't worry though, she's lovely really and she's being really kind to me."

"Alright son. I'll be back with you for good just as soon as I can get out of hospital, although I haven't the foggiest how long that'll be. And don't worry, as soon as I can I'll tell someone about your leg."

"Thanks dad. Bye. I love you." Again I was overcome by emotion, but Zak knew exactly what I was feeling.

A few days later I came out of coma, and after that I couldn't leave my body any more. I was stuck with it.

dead man talking

Of course one of my first visitors was Jocasta. She'd arranged for me to have my own private room, and had popped in a few times to leave flowers, talk to the doctors and so on, but this was the first time I was going to have to speak to her. I was absolutely bricking it, knowing she'd blame me for her only daughter's death, and rightly so. But I couldn't have been more wrong.

"How are you Michael?" I'd just woken up from the only *semi*-comatose state the drugs kept me in, and she was bending over the bed, smiling gently. She began to stroke my forehead. Again she seemed softer than before.

"Oh, you know, fair to middling." My voice was only a whisper through weakness and lack of use. I tried to raise a feeble smile too, to disarm her a bit. "I'd stand up and give you a hug, but I'm afraid my body doesn't seem to work any more."

"You stay right where you are." Her eyes were warm and glistening with emotion, she was being so kind, far kinder than I'd expected. But even so the bad side of me couldn't help thinking this was a pretty useless comment, even by her standards. Worse, I was waiting for the sudden change in tone. But it never came.

"I'm really sorry about your injuries, Michael. But don't you worry, we've got the best doctors around trying to sort you out."

"Thanks. But I don't expect them to be able to help me. Even I know that a severely broken neck means it's curtains for me on the body front. I'm just going to have to get used to it." There was an awkward silence that neither of us wanted to fill, although Jocasta eventually did.

"You know about Sinead too, don't you?"

dead man talking

"Yes, the doctors told me." They were going to wait for some time to gauge my mental state before breaking the news about her and about my own condition. But because I already knew the score on both counts, I'd pretended I didn't and asked the awkward questions as soon as I came round, to avoid any embarrassing slip ups later on. I didn't want anyone to know about what I'd experienced during and after the accident. They'd think I was soft in the head as well as the body.

I still had a large brace around my neck, but she managed to slide her arms round my limp shoulders and lay her head gently on my chest. This was a strange sensation because I could see her doing it – I was propped up at an angle – but I couldn't feel it. We both sobbed deeply, which at least proved that my tear ducts and eyelids still worked, until at length she brought her head up so I could see her properly again.

"I'm so, so sorry Jocasta. It was my bloody fault. I *killed* her!" Immediately a machine behind me – I guess it was a heart monitor – started bleeping quicker. Again Jocasta put her hand on my forehead and stroked it gently.

"Hush now, hush. Don't you be getting yourself all excited. It *wasn't* your fault."

"Of course it was, I..." Again the bleeping speeded up.

"Stop that now." Her tone was calm and loving, but firm. "Look, Michael love, the police weren't able to do a blood check after the accident because everyone was too busy saving your life. Sure they know you'd had a couple of glasses of wine, they checked with the restaurant and the pub. But they also checked with me that you'd had nothing before you went out, plus you'd eaten a good meal, so they accept you weren't away with the fairies. And sure

42

we all know that was your favourite bit of road and you'd have been going fast, but we also know Sinead loved it too, and that you're a fine driver who wouldn't have done anything stupid. The police said there was nothing you could've done with that truck abandoned where it was. They'll probably want to talk to you at some point, but they've already told me it's unlikely they'll be taking any further action."

Again a detailed conversation about the finer points of car control didn't seem appropriate, at least not at this juncture. And I guess a part of me was relieved to hear the police didn't think I was to blame. But another part would've loved them to throw the book at me to reinforce my sense of guilt. In any case all this was surface froth, deep inside it altered nothing. And there was another obvious and pressing question.

"What the hell was the truck doing there anyway?"

"The farmer is in pieces over it, so he is. The poor man says it gave out while he was driving it, just came to a halt. The battery was completely flat, he couldn't leave the lights on or anything. He ran off to get a tow as fast as he could, he knew it was in a dangerous spot. But you and Sinead... you were just terribly unlucky, Michael."

All I could feel at that point was relief that Jocasta seemed to be so understanding about it all. I was tired, very tired. But there was one more thing I had to do right away, and it wasn't going to be easy.

"Jocasta, look... before you go..." Spit it out man. "You've got to get Zak's leg x-rayed. His left leg."

"Why?"

"Look, please just do it for me will you? I'll explain later."

She looked completely bewildered, but she nodded and kissed my forehead as, exhausted, I slipped into sleep again.

The following day the medic who'd brought me back to life in the ambulance came to visit me. Of course I'd recognised him once already.

"Well thanks *a lot* for keeping me going when you could've given up, just because I found you a motor... I'm really looking forward to being stuck in this useless bloody body!" I blurted out, only half in jest, as he walked through the door. But almost immediately I was kicking myself – although not literally of course. This was hardly in keeping with my fear of revealing what I'd seen and heard.

"How... how did you know it was me?" He looked aghast.

"Oh... you know... just a lucky guess." Think Michael, think., and fast. "No... actually, err... someone told me you were in the ambulance that night, and had to get me going again." At least my quick wits didn't seem to have deserted me, and I hoped I was covering my tracks well enough. He seemed to relax.

"Yeah, I did, and you were a real goner as well. My mate had given up, but I says no, I know old Mike, can't give up on him, he sold me a motor."

"Less of the old, mate, less of the old." It looked like my banter was still intact too.

"Sorry," he carried on breathlessly, "but boy did I have to hammer your chest before you came back to us!" He paused for a moment, checking himself. "Really sorry to hear about your wife though. And about your own injuries."

dead man talking

I thanked him, genuinely. Not for saving me - I'd have
given anything for him to have failed at that - but for
being a decent bloke. And I couldn't blame him for doing
his job more than properly.

eleven

Those six months in hospital were bloody awful, to put it mildly. It was 1980, and on the outside Margaret Thatcher was busy turning the country into a yuppies' paradise. Inside I celebrated my thirty-fifth birthday lying motionless in bed, just the same as I spent every other day that summer. It was one long pit of despair, and if there *is* such a thing as hell I'm pretty sure it's not some place where the devil's disciples stick hot pokers up your arse. Oh no, there's plenty of opportunity to experience hell right here on earth. And I'd got mine in spades, trapped inside a body that no longer worked, with drips and bags and God knows what stuck into every part of me. But far, far worse, I was living every day in dread of the coming of night, when there were no distractions, sleep wouldn't come and guilt would envelop me like a thick, suffocating cloud.

I had plenty of visitors, after all I'd been a popular and successful bloke. And no one seemed to blame me for the crash, but then they wouldn't to my face, would they? Some of the guys from work came in, and afterwards my sales manager stayed behind to sort out how the business was to be run in my absence. I was pretty sure he'd do a good job, but also, to be honest, I really didn't care that much any more. It had been my main driving force for so long, but now that all seemed empty and hollow. I had more than enough money to last a lifetime, and more pressing things on my mind.

My mother visited me once a week at first but she, like all the others, found it very hard to keep coming. The clearer my predicament and the results of my actions became, the further I sank into the depths of despair, not wanting to talk to anyone or hear about anything. Truth be told she and I had drifted apart even before the crash, ever since I'd moved south really. And although I was her son, and she loved me and I her, the bond would never be that close again. I think we both knew it, and her visits became less and less frequent. I didn't mind.

After a while the only person I saw regularly, in fact every day, was Jocasta. She was the only one I wanted to spend time with apart from Zak, and he was always with her anyway – although sadly I couldn't communicate with him like before. She knew Sinead better than anyone apart from me, and it was a comfort to have her near. I found myself opening up to her more and more, and all the old animosities were starting to melt away. As I'd suspected straight after the crash she'd moved into our house to look after the little fellow full time, so she was seeing far less of her hippy pals, which seemed to me to be having a positive impact. She even *looked* normal these days, usually in simple jumpers or shirts and slacks instead of the bloody kaftans and all the other multi-coloured clobber she used to adorn herself with. Yet I was still worried she might be lonely and urged her to at least employ a nanny to help out, but she insisted she was fine. Now I really saw where Sinead got her stubborn unselfishness from.

But talking of Zak, what a change! He'd turned into the happiest little man alive, although that development wasn't without its complications. Jocasta had had his leg x-rayed at the hospital straight after our initial conversation, and even I was somewhat taken aback when the staff told her he had a partial break of the left tibia that wasn't healing properly. Apparently young babies are prone to these, their bones are so pliable they can bend until they fracture a bit but not clean through. So they fixed him up and in no time he was right as rain.

dead man talking

The staff could tell the break had occurred a few months before, and they'd checked his records and found out about his constant crying. Of course they accepted that accidents can happen with babies – an awkward tumble that doesn't seem that bad at the time, or whatever – and they certainly didn't suspect any sort of abuse. But Jocasta had had to give them an explanation of why she specifically wanted his *left leg* x-rayed, and like her they were even more intrigued when this turned out to provide the diagnosis for a relatively long-term problem that had had everyone completely baffled.

She fobbed them off that it was just a woman's intuition, and because he always seemed to hold that leg a little strangely when she lifted him up. And I in turn had fobbed *her* off a number of times, pretending to be tired whenever she broached the subject. But I couldn't hold out for much longer, and actually I didn't want to. I'd come to the conclusion that I needed to get this off my chest, to share it with someone, and she was the only person I knew who wouldn't think I was a complete basket case – apart from Sinead, and it was too late to talk to her.

"So come on now, you've got to spill the beans Michael. How the blazes did you know about Zak's leg?" she demanded right on cue on her next visit.

"It's a long story."

"Well, I've got all the time in the world. Do you have the *gift* all of a sudden?"

"What bloody gift?"

"You know! The second sight, the third eye, whatever you want to call it."

"Look Jocasta, I haven't the faintest idea what you're on

about, so please just shut up and listen. I know you're into all this stuff but it's all new to me, so just bear with me while I try to explain."

"Ok, ok, I'll keep quiet."

I took her right through the whole lot. How I'd floated around near the scene of the crash, seen my own body in the car, followed Sinead into the tunnel and then the light, fought with the Old Man when he told me I couldn't follow her, then come back and heard the conversation in the ambulance. Finally I told her about my little talk with Zak.

"Holy Mother of God, I don't bloody *believe* it!" she exclaimed when I'd finished. She'd cried with me when I told her about Sinead and that last loving look she gave me at the gate, but her eyes started to widen when I got onto the bit about the ambulance. By the time I was talking about Zak they were like saucers, and now I'd finished she was looking exultant and triumphant. "I always said that little fella was special, a real *old* soul, I could see it in his eyes. Always said it, in spite of his problems."

"Jocasta, according to Zak himself *all* babies are like that." She looked deflated as I cut her short. "And I'm sorry, but if you're going to help me get to the bottom of all this you need to cut the crap." My old frustrations were coming to the fore again.

"There's no need to take that tone with me young man. You might be laid up and all, but I won't be spoken to like that."

"I'm sorry. Look, I don't mean to take things out on you, but I want to find out what all this is about and I'm going to need *you* to help me. I *know* it can't all be my imagination. I mean, not only was it so real, but look at me recognising the medic in the ambulance, even though I had to cover my tracks with him. And then there's Zak's leg. Both those things happened when to any onlooker I was out for the count, yet they've both been proved correct. There's no way they're just flukes or lucky guesses, is there?"

"No, there's not Michael love. And don't you worry, I'll help you."

"Thanks." I looked at her and smiled, pleased that my little outburst hadn't done too much damage. "But there's one more thing. Please don't tell anyone else about this, not even your friends. I'm enough of a laughing stock already, without making it any worse."

"You're not a laughing stock at all, so don't you dare say you are!" I already knew not to mess with Jocasta when she had the bit between her teeth, so I just looked sheepish. "But I won't tell a soul, I promise."

Not much else happened during that time, every day merged into the next. But it was interesting that with the passing of time my experience somehow became *more* rather than *less* concrete. I stopped thinking of it as strange and started accepting it as fact. Indeed it seemed to have triggered some sort of *inner knowing*, which sounds poncey but it's the best way I can describe it.

Despite this I was still massively relieved to hear Jocasta proclaiming during one of her last visits that, apparently, I wasn't alone! She'd just read an article in a magazine about an American psychiatrist called Moody who, several years previously, had made a big splash with a book about people who'd had similar experiences to my own – with the tunnel and the light and so on. Apart from

dead man talking

Zak's recovery and her own kindness towards me, this was the first good news I'd had since the crash, and it really excited me. I wasn't a loony after all!

She promised to get hold of a copy of the book for when I came out, as something for me to look forward to and to spur my recovery on. And this was the one thing that gave me some hope. At least if I was going to be stuck like this I wanted to have something more than just the stifling guilt to occupy my mind. Maybe when I got home I'd be able to make some sense of everything that had happened, and especially answer the questions that burned inside me.

Why had Sinead been taken from us all so young, and was my having to remain here as a cripple some sort of punishment for killing her?

twelve

Saul knew the pain would never leave him. His guilt was total.

The whole community was in a state of shock. As the last poor wretch was dropped into nothingness the merciful crack of her neck breaking rent the air – unlike the others, who had both writhed in agony for some time before death ended their suffering. The final cheer went up, then died just as fast. Gradually everyone turned away and returned to their homes slowly, in silence. It was as if, during that last act of the whole gruesome play, the scales had been lifted from their eyes.

There were no more trials, but things did not return to normal. The children who had supposedly been bewitched became silent and withdrawn. To a hardy few this proved they had been released from possession by the women's deaths, but the majority realised it was due to shock at just how far their play acting had led.

In fact the whole community became withdrawn, and no one more so than Saul. He lay on his bed day after day, not eating or washing or doing anything except staring at the ceiling. No one had the courage to visit or check on him, not even his closest friends. After all, like him they knew his wife had been right. And instead of showing support they had hanged her, while he had done nothing to stop them. So what could they say to him, or him to them?

thirteen

When I finally came out of hospital life improved, but it was still hardly a bed of roses. I was no longer hooked up to anything, apart from the bags concealed inside my clothes that catered for my bodily waste, so Jocasta could push me around in my wheelchair. And over time I was no longer being pumped quite so full of drugs, so I was more alert.

My main internal injuries had all been in the abdominal area, where I'd rebounded into the steering wheel after slamming into Sinead as we hit the truck broadside on. My ribs and punctured lungs had mended but my breathing remained shallow, my kidneys had suffered some trauma but seemed to be stabilising, and they'd removed my ruptured spleen. The big ongoing threat was that my liver had been irreparably damaged, and was going to get gradually worse. I was on a special diet, alcohol was out, and even the mildest exertion tended to exhaust me. None of us knew quite how long I had but clearly I wasn't going to live into ripe old age.

That suited me fine, I didn't want to live long like this anyway, I wasn't only physically broken but mentally too. But in the meantime I had to make the best of it, and one major comfort was that at least I could now watch Zak growing up properly, and spend some time with him. In some ways it still frustrated me that we couldn't communicate the way we had when I wasn't in my body, but we still seemed to share a special bond. Of course I longed to pick him up, to play with and cuddle him, but at least Jocasta would sometimes lay him on my knees and I'd talk to him – although now it was all rather one-sided.

Speaking of Jocasta, she was turning into a true angel.

dead man talking

Nothing seemed to be too much trouble even after Zak started to crawl, at which point like all toddlers he was inquisitive about everything and a real handful. She also dealt with me superbly, even though I was often miserable and demanding.

But at mine and my doctor's insistence we did hire a trained nurse who lived in with us, mainly to look after my medication and do the really hard stuff – getting me out of bed in the morning, bags changed, washed, clothed and so on, and then undressing me and putting me back again at night. I didn't want a woman because, although I was a lot lighter than before, there was still some weight to me that had to be lifted in and out of beds, chairs and so on. And I wouldn't have wanted a woman to do all the intimate things he had to do. Somehow I felt I'd keep my dignity better with a man.

Jocasta had brought a few candidates into the hospital to meet me and I'd decided on a tall, skinny, slightly nerdy lad called Ken. He was only in his mid-twenties but a highly qualified carer for the severely injured and terminally ill, both from a medical and a psychological perspective. He passed his two-week probation period and I found him easy to get along with, but I still wanted him to keep himself to himself. So except when he was attending to my needs he spent his days in the rooms I'd given him upstairs. He also had one day and night off every week, which was enough, he was being *very* well rewarded.

While I was in the hospital I'd also had a stair lift fitted, thinking I'd retain some sense of normality by still sleeping upstairs. But it soon proved to be too much of a strain on all of us, and in any case I found I hated sleeping in that room without Sinead, it brought back too many painful memories. So we converted the downstairs study into a bedroom, which had the added bonus that I could lie propped up in bed and look out through the French windows at the garden.

In fact the garden became a source of real pleasure. I'd never had time to appreciate it properly before, but now I'd stare out at it for hours on end. And the weather had to be *really* cold or wet for me not to be wheeled out across the lawns for at least an hour or two, even if I had to be heavily wrapped up so as not to catch a chill.

I was particularly drawn to the huge old trees, although when I'd bought the house I'd been thoroughly unimpressed by the agent's insistence that they formed a unique and beautiful collection, including some rarities imported from abroad. Yet now I'd ask to sit by a different one each day. Yes I know I'm probably starting to sound like one of Jocasta's old hippy pals myself, but somehow there was a fascinating aura around each of these wonderful old survivors who'd lived through so much change. And yes, I probably *would've* hugged them if I could. As for the flower beds, I'd always employed a top gardener to keep the place looking good, but now at last I was appreciating his efforts. I'd spend hours by each one just drowning myself in the contrast and intensity of the colours and fragrances – for the first time realising that the magnificence of nature always far outstrips anything we create artificially.

Don't let all this apparent contentment fool you, the underlying guilt was still every bit as strong as it had ever been. But over time I'd learnt to control it a little at least, so that it no longer intruded on my *every* thought and deed or stifled *all* creativity.

Of course as soon as I got home I was keen to embark on

the journey I'd promised myself in hospital – the quest to understand what had happened to Sinead and I, and even more *why* it had happened. I wanted to get on with Moody's book, which was waiting for me as Jocasta had promised. She'd already read it and was *bursting* to discuss it, but I banned her until I'd had a chance too.

I could just have asked her to read it again aloud, but especially with this sort of stuff I wanted to do it myself, to go at my own pace and have time to think things over. As a gadget man I'd already anticipated all this while in the hospital and, as well as the stair lift, I'd ordered a complicated electronic contraption that turned the pages of a book for you. But these devices were quite new, and the bloody thing kept turning over too many at once or none at all, which drove me nuts. So after one too many visits by an engineer I politely suggested he might like to take it away and keep it – which, in as much as I made no further suggestions as to where he might like to *put* it, showed that the new, gentler me was making considerable progress.

In fact I'd already reverted to the non-technical solution, a mouthstick. As the name suggests it's a thin, light stick with a y-shape that fits inside your mouth, and with a little practice this proved a doddle. Not only that but it was reliable, and I could turn lots of pages at once if I wanted to go back and check something or look at a reference. I didn't even have to be indoors in front of a table any more, but could have my reading material resting on a special tray that fitted onto the arms of my chair.

Practicalities sorted, I was absolutely spellbound as I got through the book as fast as I could – although this wasn't so quick to begin with, I'd get mentally tired quite quickly and I'd never been a great reader anyway, so it all took a bit of getting used to. But Jocasta was right, it had stories from scores of people who'd had what were being referred to as *near-death* experiences. And there was real consistency between theirs and mine. They'd nearly all found themselves floating outside their normal body but still with some sort of less substantial one, and felt really free and light. They'd nearly all gone into the tunnel and then on into the light at the end, where they'd had that same incredible feeling of love that had knocked me off my feet. And they'd nearly all met up with a dead friend or relative who'd told them they had to go back because they still had things to do – although just like me they weren't told what.

This perked me up no end. However much I'd already accepted my experience was real, this really did reinforce my sense that I wasn't mad, and it was such a comfort to know I wasn't alone. Of course Jocasta and I had long discussions about it all too, including one evening before my bedtime when Ken knocked and stepped into my room. I was still very guarded about my experiences, but I knew he'd seen the book on my wheelchair and lying around. So far he'd said nothing out of politeness, but the subject was going to have to come up sooner or later and, since I was growing to like and trust him, I didn't send him away.

"Jocasta thinks I ought to write to Dr Moody," I said, nodding towards the book on my bedside table. "Of course I can't actually write, but I guess that's only a minor problem." I was smiling, this sort of banter kept me going.

"Mind if I take a look?" he said.

"Be my guest."

He picked it up and spent a few moments scanning the

back cover, although I got the feeling he'd probably checked it out before anyway. "Is this what happened to you, Mr Prior?" I hesitated, the words that would let someone else in on my secret still seeming to stick in my throat.

"Yes Ken... yes it is."

"Would you mind sharing your experience with me, I'd be interested?"

"Sure, why not?" I glanced at Jocasta and she gave a subtle nod, she obviously trusted him too. I gave him a quick rundown, but not the full details. "But you're only the second person that knows about all this, so please don't say anything to anyone else."

"Of course not, Mr Prior."

"Now I've told you all that I think you'd better start calling me Michael, don't you?"

"Ok Michael, whatever you say." He sat staring into space for a moment, as if deciding whether to say something.

"So what do you think of our intrepid cosmic explorer then Ken?" Jocasta put in. Again he hesitated, looking slightly awkward.

"Permission to speak freely?" He was clearly nervous.

"Permission granted." I smiled, trying to put him at ease.

"I've read a bit about this before. When I was training we covered patients who have cardiac arrests, and it came up. Forgive me, but I come from a scientific background, and they *have* been able to explain what you experienced using their understanding of brain chemistry."

"Ok, let's hear it Kenny boy, but keep it simple, I'm no brain surgeon myself." As a grounded man who still believed in the practicalities of life, I was genuinely interested to hear what he had to say. I also knew he was *very* bright.

"Well, when the brain is highly stressed, say in the type of accident you had, it produces chemicals called endorphins as an automatic reaction. These are deliberately designed to make you feel euphoric, to counter the stress. That's why you felt the way you did, and the other bits were just your imagination working overtime." This was interesting, and I sat and considered it for some moments. But it didn't seem to do a very good job of explaining the totality of my experience.

"Not sure about that. I know I didn't exactly feel euphoric at the beginning, when I looked down and saw what I'd done. Now, ok, I did start to feel a little disoriented and detached when I realised I was dead, and I felt *fantastic* when I emerged into the light and saw my Old Man, so that bit definitely fits. But euphoric is hardly the word I'd use for my reaction to being told I had to come back and leave Sinead behind."

"Exactly!" Jocasta had been listening patiently but she was hardly impartial, and you didn't have to be a genius to tell she didn't want Ken to come out on top.

"But the brain behaves in strange ways, we're only just starting to realise how incredibly complex it is." Ken wasn't looking smug, just genuine. "If I had to put money on it I'd bet that one day soon all those other aspects of your experience will be explainable, without having to resort to the idea that your consciousness was somehow operating separately from your body and brain." Again I thought for a moment before responding.

"I understand your desire for a rational, logical explanation

dead man talking

Ken, and I like to think I'm still very much a realist myself. But there's a problem with your arguments that I suspect no amount of time is going to resolve." I paused for maximum effect. I was starting to enjoy this.

"I'm all ears." Ken smiled and sat forward, while Jocasta was like an excited puppy. She'd worked out what was coming before I took him through all the details of recognising the medic in the ambulance, and of the diagnosis of Zak's leg. Even as I was still talking I could see Ken's brain was whirring away as he desperately sought an explanation for these *verified* aspects. At length he sat back in his chair.

"Couldn't you be mistaken about some of this? For example, perhaps you overheard someone talking about who'd saved your life while you were a bit drowsy when you came out of coma, and just forgot about it?" I had to think about this for a few moments, before I realised it didn't make sense in my case.

"Nice try Kenny boy, but the guy was a vague acquaintance from my old local when I first moved down this way. I only ever knew his first name, and back then he wasn't even a medic. I only knew who he was because I recognised his *face*." Now it was Ken's turn to look perplexed, but he recovered pretty quickly.

"Ah, but they could've also mentioned about you selling him the car in the conversation you overheard. It's an obvious detail to include, after all that's why he worked so hard to save you in the first place. Then the moment he came in the room you recognised him like you said you do all your past customers, even if you can't put a name to them, and straight away your subconscious linked him with the story you'd overheard."

dead man talking

This did stop me in my tracks somewhat. His explanation was certainly *possible*, but was it really *likely?* On reflection it wasn't, not in the way he meant it, because the medic came to see me so soon after I came round. But he didn't know that I'd heard a lot of what was going on in my room even when I was in coma, which allowed a lot more time for me to have heard something. And I couldn't be bothered to get into that discussion with him.

"Ok Ken, I'll accept that you just *might* be right about that part, although I still think you could be clutching at straws." I was now building up to play my trump card. "But how would you like to explain me knowing about Zak's leg?" He sighed. He knew this one had been coming.

"Now that, I have to admit, is a hard one."

fourteen

For the next few months Jocasta kept on at me about getting in touch with Dr Moody. She was absolutely right that his book contained nothing like my case in terms of its *verifiable* aspects, especially Zak's leg.

Even Ken had been flummoxed by that one, and he'd been unable to come up with anything even remotely plausible as an explanation since – although that hadn't stopped him trying. Actually I respected that he was a committed and sincere atheist, who'd seen what orthodox religion had done in various parts of the world at various times in the supposed name of God, and he didn't like it. Coupled with that he didn't believe there was anything outside the physical, material world that couldn't be explained by science. My experience alone wasn't going to change his whole way of looking at life, and I couldn't blame him for that. After all I'd already been through a similar questioning process in hospital, but all this was much easier for me because it was more real and more immediate – I'd *lived* it, and I *knew* what had happened..

Yet I kept finding excuses not to contact Dr Moody, putting it off and telling Jocasta in no uncertain terms that I didn't want her doing it behind my back either. I didn't admit it openly but inside I knew I was scared to put my head above the parapet, and of the possible publicity. The feeling remained strong that it was bad enough I'd killed my wife and so on, without everyone walking around saying that poor old Mike Prior had become a God-botherer too.

But the quest went on. Jocasta and I liked to keep abreast of what was going on via her spiritual magazines, and this near-death stuff was certainly a hot topic. Over

dead man talking

the next twelve months two more American researchers
called Sabom and Ring published separate books, and we
ordered them, avidly studying each one as soon as it
arrived. But still they seemed to have no case as
impressively verifiable as mine.

Not only that but what still interested me far more was
the burning question of why had Sinead been taken while
I'd survived as a cripple? Understanding this remained
the one thing that might help lessen my guilt, but I still felt
no closer to an answer. Of course my own experience had
already taught me not to be scared of dying, because not
only would it not be the end but, as far as I could tell from
my brief glimpse, that loving light was a pretty special
place to hang out in. Another real comfort was the
certainty that I'd be reunited with my beloved. But, other
than having all this reinforced, I seemed to be not much
further forward.

I haven't mentioned yet that Jocasta had regularly been
trying to bring up the subject of karma with me every time
I mentioned my quest, but every time I cut her short. The
whole idea of having many lives and getting punished for
your bad deeds and so on still sounded like nonsense to
me.

That was until one night when I guess I'd been out of
hospital for a little over two years. We were sat watching
television, both tired and just thinking about an early night,
when they suddenly announced that the next programme,
The Reincarnation Experiments, would really get us
thinking. While Jocasta jumped at the first word it was
the second that grabbed my attention. Was I finally going
to hear something about past lives that wasn't all airy-
fairy mumbo-jumbo? I didn't hold out much hope but I

thought I'd keep her company all the same – and in any case there'd probably be lots of chances for me to annoy her by interrupting to insist what rubbish it all was.

Wrong again. What a stunning programme! It was about this Aussie psychologist called Ramster who used hypnosis to take people back into their supposed past lives. Nothing new there, I'd read about that in Jocasta's magazines – lots of people had been starting to get in on the act, and to me it just seemed like another bandwagon. But the difference with this guy was the lengths he went to in order to try to verify the historical information his subjects came up with.

In the film there were four of them, Jenny, Helen, Cynthia and Gwen. The interesting thing was that none of them had ever been outside Australia, but they'd all remembered details of lives in various parts of Europe. So Ramster put together a film crew and brought them all over to see what checked out.

Jenny was taken to Germany and her case wasn't very impressive, but the other three! We both sat there jaws agape, not wanting to even comment after the first few minutes in case we missed a vital detail – and that was pretty unusual for us two. But when it finished we were so excited our tiredness had evaporated, and we stayed up late into the night dissecting the amazing stories we'd seen played out. Jocasta couldn't wait to tell me her favourite.

"I really liked that last woman, Gwen. I think the fact she was middle-aged and such an ordinary, humble, down-to-earth housewife made her really endearing. And she remembering so much about her life as a young Somerset girl... when was it?"

"I think they said she was born in the mid-1700s. Rose she called herself, didn't she? Rose Duncan."

"That's right. But wasn't it incredible when she was taken to Glastonbury to see the ruins of the abbey, and she was really upset because she'd loved being there so much and she felt they'd ruined the atmosphere by cleaning it all up. And it was like she really *knew* she'd been there before, and started crying and all. Heaven preserve us, I'm almost welling up myself."

"Oh come on Jocasta, this is no time for getting all bloody sentimental. And anyway that wasn't the most important bit by a long chalk. Just think of all those other more obscure things she remembered, like the local villages that no longer exist or have changed their name, and the name of their Scottish landlord and various of his pals. And all of it was proved correct in local maps and books and stuff!"

"I know, to be sure that was incredible too, but I'm a woman Michael and I love the emotional stuff. Even a typical man like you must understand that now?"

"Of course I do, it's just the other stuff is so powerful because the information is *so* detailed and obscure! Like when she led them across miles of fields and woods to her old home, and it was just a barn tagged onto a more modern house. And she was bang on about where the main door and window had been!"

"I know, even that nutty old university professor with the posh voice they took with them to witness it all... what was *his* name?"

"Basil." We were both laughing now.

"That's the man! Even *Basil* couldn't believe it when she

got that right. It was so funny when he bent over to let her draw that sketch on his back, and then it looked all wrong at first when they went round the back and he felt really sure he'd rumbled her. But his expression when they went inside and saw the originals had been bricked up, *that* was priceless so it was."

"But what about the *farmer's* expression right at the end, that was even better! Oh no you missed that bit didn't you, you had to pop to the loo."

"That was really annoying but I was busting! When I got back I saw the farmer scratching his head and going 'I don't rightly know what to make of it' in his lovely Somerset accent, and Basil beaming away in the background with his kids. So fill me in, what happened?"

"Well you saw the bit where Gwen first led them out of Glastonbury trying to find the old cottage Rose had been taken to?"

"Yes, it was to get her foot bandaged wasn't it, she'd fallen over or something in the Abbey? And she was angry that the man's cart was loaded with those special slabs of stone stolen from the abbey that he was going to use as flagstones for his floor. I got as far as them standing by the river and her pointing at that run-down shed with the corrugated roof."

"That's right. Well it turned out she was sure that was it, and they got hold of the bemused farmer to let them look inside, but the problem was the floor was covered in decades of chicken shit! Amazingly they persuaded the poor bugger to clear it overnight – I'm not sure what they told him exactly – and then they went back the next morning to find he'd revealed a whole floor of distinctive, dark blue, granite slabs just as Gwen had described!"

"Holy Mother of God! That's incredible!" I think she was as impressed as I was by that last touch.

We talked about the other cases too, Helen's and Cynthia's, and concluded they were really just as impressive. I could feel whole new vistas of possibility opening up now, and I wanted to understand the implications.

"So what does all this mean then?"

"It means that once you accept we've got some sort of soul that lives on after we die, it would be *crazy* to think it would only live once. If that was right, how the blazes would you explain one poor little sod being born into terrible poverty with no opportunities at all, and another being born with a silver spoon in its mouth?"

"God's will?" I offered, and she laughed.

"Jesus, what a relief it is that at last you're listening to what I've been trying to tell you for years – without you immediately judging what I'm about to say and shutting me up!"

"I'm sorry Jocasta, but we all have to go at our own pace. I always associated past lives with when you and your pals seemed to talk bullshit about karma and everything, and that's why I've continued to switch off, it just didn't sit well with me at all. But now I've seen there's a rational side to the idea and good, verifiable *evidence* for it, well *now* you've got my attention. That's much more like the verifiable bits of my own experience proving I was fully conscious even when technically dead, or at least in coma."

"You're a bloody trial Michael Prior, and that's a fact."

"I've got to have *some* uses mother."

"Sure I suppose you're not *all* bad." She laughed and then sat silent for a while. When she spoke again she was more serious. "You know, I can see now why you might've been put off before. And the way you approach all this, trying to keep your feet firmly on the ground, well that's starting to grow on me. I've never really been interested in all this evidence stuff before."

"Thankyou Jocasta, that's truly gracious of you after the hard time I've given you over the years." She really wasn't such a bad old stick after all.

"Truce?"

"Truce!" She walked over and kissed me on the forehead.

"But please don't forget you've got to strike a balance too, Michael." She sat down next to me and leant forward in earnest. "You can have as much evidence as you like, and that's grand because it means you've got a defence if people try to call you an idiot or a proper softy who can't face life without God to look after him. And I'm sure it attracts lots of people who'd be put off by what you call the airy-fairy stuff in my magazines, and that's grand too. But once you get into it, real, practical spirituality is a personal and individual thing. It's how you feel, what you intend, what you say and how you say it. It's loving yourself but not in an arrogant way. It's those wonderful moments when you look at a flower and realise how lucky you are, even *you* stuck in a wheelchair. Above all, Michael, *real* spirituality is about only one thing. It's about love."

I'd never heard her talk like this before. Perhaps because I'd never properly given her the chance, perhaps because she really had changed too. Or perhaps it was a bit of both. Whatever it was these were some of the wisest words I'd ever heard, and they really made me think.

dead man talking

"So apart from my huge love for Zak, and a *bit* of love for you..." I didn't want to go overboard, and she laughed. "*Apart* from that, guilt still dominates my life, even if I don't bore you by banging on about it any more, And I guess guilt is a long way away from love, isn't it?"

"It is Michael. But that's something you'll have to think through for yourself."

I did think about it, a lot, over the coming months. I'd been opened up to the possibility that Sinead and I had lived together before, and what had happened this time might even be somehow related. But, as excited as I was by Ramster's film, I was keen to see if there was other evidence to back up the idea of reincarnation. The work of just one man, however impressive, wasn't enough to be conclusive for me. To my delight, again using Jocasta's magazines and contacts, we found there was – and it seemed to be just as impressive.

There was the well-known case of Bridey Murphy from the fifties, but no one seemed to know quite what to make of that. Rather more promising though was the work of a Welsh hypnotist called Bloxham, who'd had some interesting results with a subject called Jane who recalled a number of different lives in great detail. Apparently they'd featured in a BBC film some years before and luckily the producer, a chap called Iverson who was originally a real sceptic, had produced a book to go with it.

That was soon added to the collection and I was most intrigued by her recalling a life as a servant to a rich medieval French financier called Jacques Coeur, about whom few books exist, all in French. Amongst many other obscure details she remembered that he'd been given a beautiful golden apple studded with jewels by the Sultan of

dead man talking

Turkey. As part of his follow-up checks Iverson contacted a local historian in Coeur's home town of Bourges who, after much fruitless searching – if you'll pardon the pun – managed to find the medieval court records of his trial for treason. These listed the items confiscated after he was found guilty – and there, in the list, was the golden apple!

Equally fascinating was the research being carried out by an American professor by the name of Stevenson. He'd written several books about his work with children from around the world who seemed to suddenly come up with incredible details of their last life without needing hypnosis – which brought to mind what Zak had told me about youngsters remaining more open to this kind of stuff for a while.

Not *all* his cases were that impressive but one, involving a little Indian girl called Swarnlata, stood out for me. After much pestering her father was able to trace the home of the Pathak family she claimed to have been part of several decades before, based on her descriptions, even though it was several hundred miles away. Eventually they agreed to see her and she recognised many former family members and friends, despite them trying to actively *mislead* her. She even recalled lending her former husband 1200 rupees just before she died, something he'd told no one else about but was now astonished to be reminded of.

Again to me this seemed like really solid evidence. I was well and truly hooked.

fifteen

Thank God Jocasta had the presence of mind to record the Ramster film on video. I've watched it so many times since it's beginning to wear out, while all the details are firmly etched on my memory. But more than anything, although it was Ken's night off, I was going to really enjoy making him sit and watch it.

The trouble was whenever I tried he always made excuses. I didn't want to ruin the impact by discussing the cases first, I wanted him to see them for himself, but I was getting increasingly frustrated with the way he seemed to be shutting down on me. Finally one morning I gave in, but I'd only taken him through the background briefly when he was in like a shot.

"Michael, I can understand why you're getting excited, you've been through a lot and your own experiences are, I admit, interesting. But all this talk of past lives. These people have just picked the information up from newspapers or books, television or films, overheard conversations and so on, and then forgotten about it. The brain stores everything we're ever exposed to in our memory, it's incredible, but most of this information is inconsequential so it's stored right away in the dusty recesses where it can only be accessed via hypnosis or other altered states. But then our incredible imaginations jumble all this material together to fabricate these amazing stories of past lives. But that's all they are, *stories*. There's been proper research into this phenomenon, it's called *cryptomnesia*. So there's always a perfectly logical explanation without resorting to the paranormal."

"What, just like my experience with Zak's leg?" I admit I

was goading him, but like I said he seemed to have become less open and it grated a bit. Before he could bite I carried on. "In just the same way the devil is in the detail with *these* cases, Ken. You need to appreciate just how *obscure* some of this information is."

"Ok, ok, fire away, give me an example," he sighed. I had a strong feeling that whatever I said it would make little difference. But for my own sake I really wanted to see if he could explain these cases I found so impressive. Yet I thought I'd keep my powder dry for a bit, so I started with arguably the least impressive.

"Right, this woman called Cynthia was taken to a market town in northern France called Flers. From there she was able to take the team on a several mile trip north-west into the countryside, despite lots of changes to the roads, until they came to the ruins of a magnificent old chateau that she'd recalled growing up in just before the Revolution. She said her name had been Amelie de Cheville. And they found the chateau had a really unusual tower, a lake and other features that were just as she'd described." Ken thought for a moment.

"It was a French *chateau*. I know there are plenty of them but it's hardly beyond the bounds of possibility that she'd read about it somewhere and then forgotten about it."

"What, and could take them straight to it despite some serious changes to the scenery, having described the lay of the land and the roads accurately back in Australia?"

"So the book had directions, that's really no big deal Michael."

"Hang on a minute, there's more. She also took them to a place she'd holidayed at on the coast near Mont St Michel, again finding her way along narrow country roads perfectly. She'd described the unusual internal features of a local chapel there, right down to the hexagonal stone font and the diamond-shaped, blue-grey tiles on the floor. And that's exactly what they found when they went inside."

"A little more obscure I agree, but you can hardly rule out books or films again, and a bit of lucky guesswork."

"I don't agree. I think the way she knew the directions alone was really impressive. But in case that's not enough for you, try this one for size. Another lady called Helen was taken to the centre of Aberdeen from where, again despite the massive changes to the city centre, she found her way to a college building. She said she'd been there as a medical student called James Burns in the 1830s. Not only had she drawn it in great detail while back in Australia, based on the memories triggered by her sessions with Ramster, but she knew the building inside out."

"Books or something again, it was an old building in a major city." He was becoming really dismissive.

"No, that's where you're wrong Kenneth my boy. Only *one man* knew exactly how it had been laid out way back then, and his study had never been published. Yet when he quizzed her on intricate internal details she was able to tell him exactly how to get from A to B via staircases and so on that were no longer there. He was actually a sceptic like you, but at the end he admitted he was completely at a loss to know how she could possibly have had such obscure information at her fingertips. I couldn't agree more... unless she actually *had* lived there before."

He was quiet this time, so I thought I'd press home my apparent advantage by telling him about Gwen in Glastonbury. I gave him a quick overview of the other cases from Iverson and Stevenson too. Still he remained pensive when I'd finished, so I thought I'd take my chance and hit him with a summary.

"So, only *one* other living person knew about the layout of Helen's college, while *no one* alive knew about Gwen's flagstones. Swarnlata's former husband *alone* knew about the 1200 rupees. And if that's *still* not enough for you, Iverson's golden apple was found in a French town's civic records dating back to the middle ages, and it's probable that *no one* had looked at them for hundreds of years for Christ's sake! This isn't the sort of information they could've been exposed to in any *normal* way." I'd even exhausted myself by this stage, so I paused to get my breath back. Finally Ken roused himself.

"Look Michael, all this may seem very impressive to you but these reports are just anecdotal. They can't be relied on, or the circumstances scientifically reproduced and studied under controlled conditions."

"This research may not be entirely scientific in the conventional sense Ken, but surely it's too easy to hide behind that excuse? Does that really mean the most *rational* thing to do is ignore this significant collection of anecdotal evidence, or dismiss it out of hand? Is that how our ancestors managed to push the boundaries of human knowledge, by shutting themselves off to new possibilities?"

"I still think most of the people involved in your cases are just mistaken, or even downright frauds."

"I can't let you get away with that. With these kind of cases the details are *so* obscure and impressive there's no way you can just put them down to careless mistakes or misunderstandings. That would make the people involved morons, which they clearly aren't. So I agree, the only normal explanation that might make *any* sense would have to be deliberate fraud. But there's a big problem with that."

As in our first conversation about my own experiences, I paused to build up the tension. The difference was that this time I'd been through most of these arguments in my head already. But Ken seemed a little distracted. Or was it bored? Defeated even? At any rate he said nothing, but I wasn't in the mood to let him off the hook now. I guess there were still remnants of the old, competitive Michael lurking within me.

"For fraud, you have to have motive. Now Stevenson for example is only too well aware of the possibility with child cases, especially if the former family is wealthier. But often it's clear there's no question of the child's family asking for money, even when the former family *is* wealthier. This was the case with Swarnlata, and her parents were hardly paupers anyway. As for the regression cases, people like Ramster and his peers are professional psychologists and psychiatrists, they're not going to just make stuff like that up, it would ruin them."

"They might. People do strange things." Even Ken himself didn't sound overly convinced by his response.

"Of the handful of researchers and their key subjects we've discussed, you might get the odd rotten apple Ken, although even then there'd have to be real complicity and consistency amongst all the players in that particular drama. But you can't tell me *all* of them are bent, it stretches credulity." He was silent again, staring out at the garden. Although part of me didn't like to do it, it was time for the final thrust. "If that's the best you've got, I'm afraid it's *you* who's the irrational one old son, not me."

dead man talking

Perhaps for some people, once something isn't their cup of tea, there's no changing that fact. Or perhaps he just wasn't ready to appreciate there was a clear distinction between this type of evidence-based approach to spirituality and the orthodox religion he so despised.

And yes, before you mention it, I know I sound a little different these days. But that's what happens when a kid with little formal education finally dares to believe they've got a decent brain just like everyone else.

I was hoping that Ramster might have produced a book about the women in his film, but apparently this was still in production. However he had written a more general one about his past-life work several years earlier, so we got hold of that from Australia.

It turned out to be much more relevant to my quest, because much of his time was devoted to what he called regression *therapy*. That is hypnotising subjects into past lives and then seeing the connections with problems in this one. For example, if someone had previously died by drowning they might now have a phobia of water. This was surely leading me closer to the answers I sought about Sinead and I, but of course it forced me to finally confront my *own* phobia about the idea of karma.

I knew enough from Jocasta and from picking up various snippets that the Sanskrit word karma literally meant *action*, but that most people interpreted it as some sort of law of action *and reaction*. This is the source of the everyday phrases we all use as warnings, like "be careful, remember you reap what you sow" or "don't forget, what goes around comes around". But in past-life terms they were saying that if you generate bad karma in one life by doing bad things to others, you pay for it in the next by being on the *receiving* end of bad stuff. And, conversely, if you do good things you attract good stuff to you.

So ever since I'd seen Ramster's film and started to take reincarnation seriously I'd been mulling this over. I now realised that Jocasta's banging on about being an old soul working off all her past karma had really put me off originally because it seemed to smack of ego. But even if I ignored this sort of talk, somehow the basic idea still didn't resonate.

Yet I had high hopes that someone like Ramster, doing this kind of therapy, would surely have a more sophisticated view of karma that would help me to understand what had happened to me. Sadly I was disappointed. Indeed his take seemed to be even more hardline than most, with him describing it as *exact retribution for past misdemeanours*. Blimey, on that basis I must have done something *really* bad!

In any case, again Jocasta and I found out that a number of other regression therapists from Britain and America had written books about all this, and over the coming weeks I immersed myself in them completely. Names like Cannon, Kelsey and Grant, Netherton and Fiore were never far from my lips, and poor little Zak hardly got a look in as my quest became almost obessional.

The problem was they all seemed to have this same idea, that karma is some sort of process of paying off debts – although one of them talked about debts *to yourself,* which I thought was a little more intriguing. Yet it seemed obvious to me that, just as with Ramster, the details of their very own cases in the same books told a different and far more complex story. Sometimes their patients did bad things in life after life without ever seeming to be punished, while others seemed to get the thin end of the wedge again and again and again, with no respite. Nowhere did I see any sort of alternating pattern of victim and perpetrator, which is surely what you'd expect to find if their definitions of karma were correct.

Things got even worse when I tried to apply all this to my own situation. Since I was the perpetrator this time, had I been the victim before and now I was getting my retribution in? But then having killed Sinead I was saddled with huge guilt, so wasn't I more like a victim anyway, especially since I was crippled too? If so, perhaps this was some sort of *immediate* retribution? Or was it just a new cycle of bad karma I'd just created for myself that I'd have to pay for in a future life? If so would Sinead and I have to come back together again so she could do to me what I'd done to her? Or would it be enough that I was killed by someone else? Or could they just do something really bad to me, but not kill me? Either way, what would that mean for *their* karma? And what about the impact all this had had on those around us, like Zak and Jocasta, and their karma?

The questions just went on and on, and I could find no answers, only more questions. When it came to a specific, difficult case like ours, Jocasta too was forced to accept that the sort of general platitudes about karma that had tripped so easily from the tongues of her hippy pals didn't even scratch the surface.

Intuitively I *knew* there must be more to it. But I was slowly becoming convinced that the answers might not be found in this world.

sixteen

Saul knew he was close to death. He'd hardly eaten for nearly six weeks and his body was wasting away. But he also knew that even this penance would not save him from keeping a sure and certain appointment with Satan himself. His failure to defend his wife, when *she* had been the one following God's true path all along, had been so abject that the fires of hell could burn forever and hardly touch the deep, dark stain on his soul.

seventeen

So, here I am again. I'm ready.

I guess I was holding my own for the first four years or so after I came out of hospital, but in the last six months I've really started to go downhill. I've become increasingly jaundiced as my liver has slowly deteriorated, and I've had less and less energy even for the few things I used to enjoy – my garden, playing with poor little Zak, reading, even discussing the meaning of life with Jocasta and Ken.

Truth be told it's been a real struggle. Like I said I don't like to be shown a mirror any more but I know I look really sick, and my skin has probably got an even more deathly, yellow pallor than when it last confronted me. So I'm ready to go, I want to go. I've done everything I can down here, now I want some real answers.

Jocasta and I always agreed that when this time came we wouldn't try to prolong things, and I've always been adamant I want to die at home. Although I've been back on increasing doses of drugs that make me drowsy again most of the time, at least I've been here, in my own bed, looking at my own garden, getting ready in my own way. And it feels fine.

There's a part of me that doesn't want to leave Zak of course, but I know he'll continue to love Jocasta as the only mother he's ever really known, and she him. And it's not as if I'm much use to him any more. I can't even bear his weight on my lap for more than a few seconds now, it just exhausts me even if he does stay still, which is asking a lot of an active five year old. As for Jocasta herself, although she's never protested and we've become really close, at last she'll be freed up to have some sort of a life instead of having to be my guardian angel all the time.

It might sound harsh but I know I won't really miss them once I'm gone. I've already had a taster of that different perspective you have on the other side, where you're more detached from earthly concerns. It saddens me more to think about how *they* might react to me being gone from *their* lives, because it's the people left behind who suffer most – although not so much if they understand that death isn't an ending at all, and we all get to meet up again.

On that basis I think Jocasta will be fine, but I've tried to reassure Zak that he'll see me again in heaven one day. Yet every time he seems to be amazingly cool about it. In fact his replies have that world-weary honesty that children do so well: "Daddy, I do love you and I will miss you, but I *know* about all that. You don't have to keep *telling* me." Whatever I might have said to Jocasta while in hospital, she's right, he really *does* seem to be quite special.

Another thing that tells me it's time to go is that over the last few months I've been finding myself out of my body again. It seems to happen automatically when I'm dosing, and I don't go very far, I just float around my room. But the one thing I've seen that I don't recall being aware of before is this kind of silvery chord that connects my two bodies. It doesn't restrict where I can go, but I've realised it has a far more important function – it's what keeps my physical body *alive*. So if I want to leave *before* my body completely gives up I've got the option just to go to sleep, wait until I find myself outside it, then snip! sever the chord and I'm off.

And now that I've said my goodbyes, and everything is in order, that's exactly what I'm going to do. I guess my body might continue to function for a while, maybe even a few days, but it won't be me. If you look into my eyes you'll see they're dead, because I won't be in there any more.

Free at last! FREE AT LAST!!

PART TWO

eighteen

Michael. He was a good guy. Not perfect of course, but who is? I like him, but he wasn't me – merely an *aspect* of me. Is that confusing? I promise I'll do my best to explain, but it may take a little time, so please be patient my friend.

After I severed Michael's chord – my chord – I was far more prepared than when I temporarily died in the crash. But of course it's ridiculous to use the word *died* now, because you've realised that I'm not dead at all. I'm still very much alive. In fact much more alive now than I ever was in my physical body. Much more.

I did decide to hang around for a few days, although to me it felt like no time at all. One thing I should explain is that time is very different where I am now, you *feel* it differently. Things that might take weeks, months or even years for you can fly past in the blink of any eye here. But there's still some sense of continuity, of events that happen one after the other, of cause and effect.

Of course a part of me wanted to press on into the light as fast as possible to find Sinead. But I was also curious to see who'd turn up for my funeral, and how they would react. You see at the end I'd finally agreed with Jocasta that once I was gone she could have free reign to say anything she liked about my experiences during and after the crash, our quest together and so on. Although I'd never followed up on her suggestion I should contact Dr Moody, and she'd given up on pressing me about it, an inner voice had been increasingly nagging away at me that my story was important not only for me but for other people as well. And although I'd continued to lack the gumption or energy to say anything about it publicly myself, I'd at least accepted that others should be able to learn from what had happened to me after I'd gone, if they chose to.

So I wanted Jocasta to tell everyone I'd had first-hand experience that you don't die when your body does, and that they shouldn't mourn for the already-decrepit flesh that lay in the coffin before them. That even though my life was cut somewhat short and had been a real trial after the crash, it had been very good before that, so they should celebrate it in its totality rather than dwell on its more recent tragedies. And that, as far as we could tell, not only would I see my beloved Sinead again but, sooner or later, I might even come back to haunt them again in another body.

I also wanted her to emphasise the elements of my experiences that produced information I couldn't possibly have acquired by any normal means, which of course meant opening up about my communication with Zak when he was still just a baby. We had tried to discuss this with him subtly in those last few months, knowing it would be brought up at the funeral, but he seemed to have no memory of it – which was pretty much in keeping with what he himself had told me at the time about young children progressively losing their special memories and awareness.

I wanted my body burnt at the local crematorium. If it had been of little use to me in the later years of my life it was even less use now, and I felt strongly that people who wanted to should remember me in their hearts at any time, not feel obliged to visit a cemetery somewhere on a regular basis to tend a grave.

In any event I was pleased to see how many people turned up to pay their respects – we don't lose all sense of ego after we pass over you know, at least not straight away. It seems I was still talked about because of the successful business that continued to bear my name, and my deliberate isolation after the crash hadn't stopped them remembering the old me with some fondness.

I was even more pleased that Jocasta's eulogy was superb. Compared to how she was when I first met her, her deep inner spirituality was now coming right from the heart, without her having to wear it on her sleeve. On top of that it was now combined with a groundedness and confidence that had turned her into a truly impressive spiritual force.

But how would all this talk of my experiences go down with the assortment of car dealers, customers and other friends and acquaintances I hadn't seen for years? As far I as I knew few of them would ever talk about anything other than cars, money, houses, holidays and possessions. Yet Jocasta – who was, after all, the one now taking the risks – had already told me not to be so judgmental, and to wait and see. And how right she was.

The drinks were flowing freely at the celebrations, held in a special marquee erected in the garden of the White Hart. And as I drifted around eavesdropping I found many people were not only reminiscing about cars I'd sold them or scary test drives I'd taken them on or good times we'd had together, but also discussing my experiences. Admittedly with some astonishment, but not dismissing them out of hand. I was relieved that at last some good might come of the crash after all.

At last even I'd had enough of listening to myself being talked about, and was ready to leave properly. I saw that Jocasta was briefly alone, so I grabbed my chance and floated over to her to whisper one last goodbye and thankyou. This was one bit we hadn't planned, indeed I hadn't even told her I'd attend my own funeral because I hadn't been absolutely sure I'd be able to control what happened that much. But as it turned out I had as much control over what I did and where I went as I'd had in my physical body. More in fact. In any case I'm fairly confident she picked my message up. She definitely stopped worrying about everyone else for a moment and paused, staring into space with a slight frown before letting a barely perceptible smile play at the corners of her mouth.

Then I moved closer to Zak, who was running around like a mad thing and being fussed over by everyone – but taking it all in his stride, of course. When he finally stayed still for a moment I bent down and whispered a final goodbye in his ear too. And he too seemed to smile to himself. Was it my imagination, or did I pick up a faint unspoken response?

"Bye-bye daddy. I love you."

nineteen

As soon as I decided I wanted to move on into the light, I felt something quite different from when I died previously. I thought I'd just float up and find my way into the entrance to the tunnel again, but I didn't really see a tunnel at all.

Describing all this isn't easy using normal language because we're now talking about operating without a physical body, and with a totally different perspective on time and space and everything else too. But the best way I can try to explain is that I had this incredible sensation of speed. Yet I'm not convinced I was actually moving anywhere, it felt more like I was upping my level of vibration, for want of a better word, as if my whole awareness was speeding up.

I also had this sense of getting not just *faster* but *lighter* too, as if I was progressively shedding much of the heaviness and denseness of earthly life with all its myriad concerns. I think this explains the general feeling of no longer caring and of detachment that I'd also had the previous time. And again there was the ever more intense feeling of being surrounded by unconditional love, which was absolutely overwhelming to start with. But that itself was almost expressed as light, so it was just speed and lightness and love all combining into this indescribable experience of shifting up through layers of energy – just like shifting up through the gearbox of the old Porsche, but far, far more pleasurable still.

So there were some similarities with the previous time, but also some major differences. Whether this was simply down to my having a clearer perception, or to them being genuinely different experiences because first time round I wasn't really moving on, I honestly couldn't say. What I can say is that this time it felt even more incredible.

I needed a little time to reacquaint myself with being in the midst of this brilliant, loving, all-encompassing light – a bit like adjusting your eyes when you've been in a dark room and suddenly emerge into bright sunshine. Indeed there was no sense of urgency, I could happily have bathed in that radiant shower of pure energy forever. But after a while I became aware of another ball of light even more intense than its surroundings heading in my direction, and gradually it took the form of the Old Man. Here he was again to meet me!

We hugged as before but somehow this time I seemed to have a little more understanding of what was going on. It was as if one minute we were some sort of nonphysical replicas of who we had been, then the next we were just balls of pure energy dancing around and mingling and merging with each other, even becoming one, before separating again.

"Look, dad, I'm sorry about what happened that last time, but this time can I *please* see Sinead?"

"Of course, son, of course. But no more trying to give me a smack, ok? Even if you can't make contact with your fist it's the intention that counts, and we don't take too kindly to that sort of behaviour around here." His hearty laugh was just as I remembered it, and I joined in.

"Don't worry on that score old son. I'm a bit better prepared and a bit calmer this time." He took my hand and immediately we seemed to emerge into a room. As I took in my surroundings I slowly recognised the main bar of the White Hart. Somehow it felt right to be here, although a little confusing as well. He led me towards the table in the corner by the fireplace, where my beloved and I had sat that night before the accident. A girl was sitting alone with her back to us. Her long, auburn hair tumbled down over her shoulders...

"Sinead, my love!" She turned round, beaming from ear to ear. Oh my God, oh my God, oh my God, I'd been so sure we'd have this reunion but it was still such a rush that it was actually happening at last! I threw myself at her and we held each other tight. Once again that feeling of merging, of pure oneness, washed over me – if it's possible seeming even more intense this time. There's simply no earthly description that would do it any sort of justice. To refer to it as the most pure, transcendental, blissful, even orgasmic togetherness and understanding would be like trying to describe a sea of brilliantly hued flowers to someone who only understood black, white and grey.

When we finally separated and all three of us were sat down I was speechless – yes, even telepathically speechless. I just couldn't imagine feeling any more contented or at peace than sitting at *that* table in *that* pub, with the woman I loved so much and had so desperately missed for five long years, and with the Old Man, the best friend I'd ever had.

Finally I stopped beaming like a demented Cheshire cat and composed myself. Somehow it didn't seem right to bring up the crash, despite my previous inability to let it go and impatience for answers.

"So is this what heaven's like then?"

"Kind of." Sinead's knowing, teasing smile didn't seem to have changed at all, although hard as it is to credit she seemed to be even more beautiful than before. I had to make a real effort to turn my attention back to the Old

dead man talking

Man. I looked properly this time and he seemed to be younger somehow, more my sort of age.

"Have you got age-reversing pills up here or something?"

"Son, round here you can be any age you want. In fact, any*body* you want." As he said this, his appearance morphed into that of a swashbuckling young pirate, replete with eye patch and bandana. My amazement and confusion was hardly lessened when I turned back to find Sinead was now an ancient priestess of some sort, wearing a beautiful white robe and stunning gold jewellery.

"What are you two doing?! Who are you?" Yet even as I said this I felt some sort of recognition of both of them.

"All in good time, son, all in good time." What had been the Old Man grinned and made desperate efforts to wink at me with his one good eye, but it was pretty obvious his attention was being diverted by something behind me – no matter how much he was desperately trying to ignore whoever or whatever it was. I turned round.

It wasn't immediately obvious why a man who not only looked like that guy from that television show who creeps up from behind and surprises you, but quite clearly *was* that guy, should be directing his slightly sheepish, lop-sided grin at me, big red book tucked underneath his arm, building up the tension before delivering his infamous line.

"Michael Prior, *this* is *your* life." My two table companions started clapping and hooting wildly.

"Oh come on, this is a joke. I'm not famous!" I pleaded, my embarrassment rising as I realised the bar had filled up and everyone had turned round to watch events unfold.

"Everyone gets on the show *here*." The TV man still had that ridiculous grin on his face. "Are you coming?"

twenty

As I followed the TV man across the bar everyone started clapping and cheering. I even seemed to recognise many of them, although I had no time to put names and places to the faces. We walked through the front door but, instead of the others following us through as I'd expected, he closed the door behind me. Seeing my mounting discomfort he beckoned me to sit down next to him on a bench, underneath one of the big umbrellas.

"What on earth is going on? Unless there've been some very recent developments that I know nothing about, you're at the height of your popularity and you're not even dead yet! And why aren't Sinead and the Old Man and all those others joining us anyway?" This felt like some sort of trick, and all my euphoria was starting to evaporate fast. Had the Old Man and even Sinead been impostors? Was there really a separate hell after all, and was I just about to find out what it was really like?

As if to answer all my questions the TV man began to change, and as he did so he seemed to tap into a reservoir of energy and understanding deep inside me, releasing it. I suddenly found myself sat next to a figure that was even more familiar to me, her beautiful eyes radiating a love that I now remembered only too well. Her long, sliver hair surrounded a smiling face that was both timelessly young and beautiful, and contained the wisdom and experience of all the ages, all at the same time.

It was my spirit guide, Aya. At least that's what her name approximates to using our alphabet. She, I instantly knew, had been around to assist and instruct me with this sort of transition many times before, and she had a predilection for playing practical jokes on her charges –

me in particular because I like to think of myself as a bit of a comedian. Yet again I'd just been had to some effect.

"You absolute cow!" She had completely collapsed now, and once again I merged with her in a sea of love and laughter.

At length I separated from our joyous reunion and this time we both remained more like spheres of bright light and energy. Our surroundings too no longer had that sense of the physical they'd had when we walked out, we were just *being* in the light, and I realised – or remembered – that now I could control how I projected myself and how my surroundings looked just as much as the Old Man, Sinead and Aya had. At first they'd simply worked with my subconscious to thought-create the whole pub scene, to make me feel at home on my return, and to make my transition into these energetic realms a little easier. Obviously that's what had best suited me as Michael, but most people are rather more cultured. They find themselves in the middle of beautiful vistas – sandy shores by turquoise seas, flower-strewn meadows, ice-capped mountains, crystalline castles in the clouds – whatever takes their fancy. But don't think too badly of me for the pub thing, I'm sure other aspects of me have experienced beautiful scenery like that after other lives.

So now I reawakened to what the Old Man had meant when he said we can be anyone we want here. To start with he and Sinead projected and I perceived the most familiar characteristics of who they were in the life we just shared – although he was obviously being a little vain when he lowered his age compared to how I most remembered him. Then to help me to open up they'd morphed into people I'd had other lives with – I now *knew* everything about how he and I'd been pirates together several centuries before, and about how I'd been Sinead the priestess' secret lover somewhere in the East back in a very distant epoch. But after we reacclimatise most of us stop projecting any sort of earthly form unless there's good reason. Instead we just perceive each other as the concentrations of pure energy we really are.

Aya was of course aware of the high-speed refresher course I'd just given myself, and was ready to help with any queries that arose during my reorientation.

"You know when you took me outside just now, for a moment I really panicked. I thought I'd gone to hell! I know now I haven't... not unless you're suddenly going to sprout horns?" I waited, but she just looked bemused. "Ok, ok, but for what it's worth just remind me, is there such a thing? And if so, pardon the pun, but having killed Sinead why the hell aren't I in it?"

"Well, what do *you* think?" As I should've expected she was throwing my own question right back at me. She knew I already had all the answers if I made the effort to reconnect with them, and wasn't about to make it easy for me.

"I suppose if we create what we perceive after we die then some people might expect to go to hell or see demons so much that they'd actually conjure them up. And if enough dead people did that, over time their projections would become a sort of reality they all shared, which in turn would attract others who felt the same way. And I guess this could be true of any number of these sorts of realities people make for themselves to inhabit after they die. But as real as they seem to those caught up in them, underneath it all they're no more real than you pretending to be that chap off the television just now. All they'd have to do was see right through the illusion and instead set the intention to be right in the heart of the light, where all falsities and projections melt into nothing."

"Not bad, not bad, you're still as sharp as ever... even though you've just had a pretty rough ride." She wasn't being sarcastic, she was showing genuine concern. "So come on, why didn't *you* end up in any kind of hell?" That one was easy.

"Because I didn't believe in it in the first place."

"Exactly. And you'd already put yourself through a kind of hell anyway, hadn't you?" This jerked me back to the personal issues that had been pressing so heavily upon me only a short time before.

"Well, apart from my own injuries, killing and losing Sinead was a real rough one. I haven't talked to her about it yet, it didn't seem right when we were so happy to see each other. But now you've reminded me I still don't seem to be able to forgive myself for what I did to her."

Clearly I hadn't left *all* my earthly concerns behind, because a sharp emotional pain such as I'd felt so often after the crash was suddenly piercing me again, for the first time since I'd left my body – and in an instant my whole life was flashing before me in the minutest and most vivid detail. It felt like I was actually *reliving* it exactly as it happened, yet it was all over in the blink of an eye.

Another veil had been lifted as I recognised this as a familiar process I'd been through many times before. Yet there did seem to be a difference this time. Normally it would make me feel considerably better, even when it became obvious there were things I'd badly messed up, because I'd immediately be able to put everything into the right sort of perspective and any negative emotions left would just fade away. But this time the guilt was still very much alive and kicking. There was no doubt I suddenly had a far clearer understanding of a great many things about that life, even including long-forgotten incidents – both good and bad – from my earlier years. But I still wasn't properly getting to grips with the more recent, tragic events. It seemed as though my feelings of guilt continued to throw a blanket of fog over them.

Aya understood exactly what was happening, and told me to put all my focus into those very feelings. And as I did so she disappeared, and everything began to change again.

twenty one

When the great day arrived Zak was still up and down and the one babysitter she had some confidence in, her mother, was confined to bed with a heavy cold. As far as Sinead was concerned no one else would do and, although I could understand that, I was still massively disappointed for both of us. And she could tell.

"I'm really sorry my love, I just can't leave him. But I want you to go out, you need it too." This was so typical of her, her unselfishness was total, and there was no hint of her saying it to test me.

"I can't go out without you, it's *your* thirtieth birthday for Christ's sake! And I don't *want* to go out without you either. The whole point of this was for the two of us to be together, to have a little quality time at last."

"I know that and I'd have loved it too, but I have to stay. We'll celebrate my birthday together when Zak is better, ok? But in the meantime I'm putting my foot down, Michael. You've been looking forward to this even more than I have, and you need it more than I do. You've got all the pressures of work as well, and I know you, you need to let your hair down every now and then, whereas I don't. Just go to the pub, see some of your mates and enjoy yourself. Go on, do it!" I knew better than not to follow orders when she was like this and, although I hated the thought of going without her, I did need to relax and unwind with a few drinks.

"Ok, but I'm not staying out late."

"You stay out as late as you want. In fact if you come home before twelve I'll kick your backside."

dead man talking

I kissed her deeply, hugged poor little Zak and walked out to the waiting Black Beauty. Its aggressive lines still made my blood pump, it was the perfect antidote to stress.

"We'll have some fun tonight, you and me."

I drove to our local, the White Hart. Although I sometimes took customers there for lunch, I hadn't been there for a proper evening out for a long time. I received a jovial reception when I entered the bar.

"Blimey, the thumb print's still there on his forehead but at least he's here! Let you out at last has she?" Sean the owner was an old friend, a wealthy man who bought all his cars from me and wasn't averse to a few drinks himself. We'd been in plenty of scrapes together before I married Sinead, and I guess he still missed those times – especially since his own more recent marriage to a much younger girl had already failed, so he was back playing the field again. He knew about the problems we were having with Zak and was genuinely sympathetic, but this was no time for a public display of sympathy.

"Yeah, well, at least I'm not a sad old git still trying to hang onto his youth. Pint of your finest lager landlord, and make it snappy, I've got some steam to let off!" We shook hands warmly, slapped each other on the back and the night was all set.

I had a great few hours with the locals then, at closing time, Sean and I decided we'd drive over to our local nightclub. We'd had a few drinks but were only going a few miles into the nearby town. I wasn't sure I'd be staying for the duration so we agreed to drive separately, and as we walked out into the car park the sight of his gleaming red Ferrari lined up next to the Beauty was bound to bring out the boys in us.

"I'm gonna give him his head on our favourite bit of country road, there's fewer people about and no law. You gonna try and follow me?"

"No way, you're a nutter over that bridge, and anyway my Italian Stallion loves big, open roads. I'll go the proper way and a fiver says I'll be ordering my drink while you're still parking!" This was, of course, way too much of a challenge for me to resist.

"Come on my Beauty, this will be easy money, like taking candy from a baby."

We sped off in different directions. But I never made it to the club. Flew over the bridge into a tight blind bend and straight smack! into the back of a farm truck parked right on the exit. I was in a bad way, my heart even stopped at one point, then I was in coma for several weeks – during which time I had a weird meeting with Zak in which he diagnosed a problem with his leg. When I came round I was paralysed from the neck down, and with internal injuries as well I had to remain in hospital for six long, tedious months.

Sinead was distraught at first, but she soon adapted and tried to make the best of things. She was intrigued by my experience with Zak and delighted that he was now better. But after I got home the strain on her was massive. She was lumbered with me as well as a growing toddler, and she still refused to let me hire any help. I tried to insist that lugging my useless frame from bed to wheelchair and back, and doing all the other things I now couldn't, was way too much for her. But she was adamant she'd care for me herself, just as she had our baby.

I'd only been out of hospital for about a year when she was taken from me. Apparently she'd had a heart defect from birth that had never been diagnosed, and she'd been straining it so badly it just gave out. I was devastated and consumed by guilt – if only I hadn't gone out by myself, if only I hadn't decided to go on to the club, if only I hadn't been driving so fast, if only I'd drunk less, if only I'd insisted on getting her some help to look after me.

Instead I'd killed her, and the pain was unbearable.

twenty two

"What on earth was that all about?" The intense guilt was stronger than ever after this latest little episode. Aya delayed her response as she let me wind down from the experience.

"You've just gone back and replayed things from a different angle."

"Did those things I've just seen actually happen?" I was completely confused, but she was smiling now. She'd switched back to projecting herself for this difficult bit of my journey, and I'd followed suit.

"Yes and no," she replied. "There are lots of things round here that aren't black and white, you ought to remember that at least." That sounded like a challenge, but I wasn't sure how capable I was of meeting it.

"Well right now I seem to have just experienced the same life, but with two different endings that felt equally real. So were they the same or not?" Loving environment or not I was struggling here and wanted some answers for a change.

"No, not as such. The version you remembered first is the one you actually lived and experienced on earth. The second was like a back-up plan if certain things had turned out slightly differently."

"So anyone can experience the back-up versions of their lives?"

"If it's useful for them, yes."

"Then what's the difference between the back-ups and the life you actually live?"

"That life is the one you really control as you go along, interacting with other people. Remember you all have free will to make whatever choices you want, even if we guides try to nudge you in certain directions sometimes. In your case Jocasta chose to babysit, but the backup was there in case she made the other decision."

"But we all make choices all the time." My head was really spinning now. "So there must be thousands... no, *millions* of back-up plans for *everyone*, and all having to *interact* with each other." Aya just smiled provocatively as she watched me taking all this in. Slowly the fog was starting to lift. "So even if I hadn't killed Sinead in the car, I'd still have killed her in some other way?"

"Understand one thing. You didn't *kill* her at all, in either situation."

"Ok, ok, but the one thing common to both alternatives was that I felt responsible for Sinead's death, and really struggled with the guilt afterwards."

"Good *boy*, now you're starting to get there." At least I knew that Aya and I often played the teacher and naughty schoolboy in these review situations, it was our way of diffusing the tension of a process that was often quite painful – for me because I was coming to terms with difficult aspects of the life I'd just left, for her because she had to wait patiently while I struggled to remember things I already knew.

"But there's a lot more to it than that," she continued." I thought for a moment, but nothing came.

"Please teacher, I need a clue." I did my best to look confused, and it wasn't that hard.

"Ok, let's go right back to square one. Do you remember the nightmare you had before Sinead died?"

dead man talking

"Yes, it was horrible. And then I saw the same scene after the crash."

"And what do you think your nightmare was designed to tell you?" Again nothing came to me.

"I dunno." I even shrugged my shoulders and looked petulant.

"Stop messing about, you know you've got to do this for yourself so don't be lazy. What happened *before* you had the nightmare?"

"Sinead and I had that awful row about Zak's education." Time to be serious, I needed to get to the bottom of this.

"Yes, but what was the row *really* about?"

"Money?"

"Sort of, but what was Sinead trying to tell you about money?"

"That it didn't matter how much we had."

"Ok, but what else had she been trying to share with you ever since you met her, which was what lay underneath her comments about money that night?"

"I guess she sometimes tried to talk to me about spiritual things, but I always switched off."

"Indeed you did. And you did so even when your intuition was repeatedly trying to tell you to listen to her. Do you remember?" Now she too was serious. There was no judgment in her tone, as always she was merely helping me make my *own* evaluations.

All of a sudden I found myself reliving multiple scenes where Sinead was trying to speak to me about such things. I even found myself in her shoes, feeling her frustration as I fobbed her off. What a jackass I'd been! Mixed in with these instant replays were all the times I'd silenced and ignored the quiet but insistent voice inside my head. Easily pushed aside while on earth, now it sounded like a veritable banshee! I realised with full and frightening force just how much I should've listened to it, and to Sinead, instead of being so preoccupied with my business, our house, the cars and all the other material distractions. It was all starting to make some sense.

"So the nightmare was a warning that if I continued to not listen something far more dramatic would happen to wake me up... I'd lose her."

"Eureka!" Even if Aya thought I'd cracked it, I wasn't so sure. Again I thought for a while but I still wasn't happy.

"That's not very fair though, is it? I mean, almost all the people I knew on earth were preoccupied with material things too, and I didn't see *them* all being crippled and losing their loved ones!"

"Calm down, calm down. Who said anything about *fair?* That's not how it works, remember?"

Another instant dose of clarity bulldozed its way into my consciousness. I *did* remember. I remembered that I'd set these tests for *myself.* That I'd actively *planned* much of what had happened with Sinead before we were even born. I'd agreed that after several hardly exemplary lives – including when I was a swashbuckler with the Old Man – I needed to remember what it was like to lead a more actively spiritual life. But the real test was choosing circumstances in which I could easily become distracted and preoccupied by the glitz and glamour of money and possessions. I also remembered that, if I'd passed this test with Sinead's help and prompting, there was much good I could've done – especially because I'd still have amassed a fair bit of money and could've used it to great effect. Not only that but, if I blew my chance the first time round, I'd be given such a shock that I'd have what was in some ways an even easier second chance to pass the test.

Of course I did blow that first chance, and my experiences after the shock of the crash did pretty much *force* me down a spiritual path. Yet still I wimped out of the chance to do something constructive with them. I could've had the guts to speak about them openly, which might have been of great benefit to others, but instead I cut myself off from the world. Admittedly I made sure Jocasta spoke about them after my death, but that was a pale imitation of what I could've achieved myself. And it wasn't being a cripple that stopped me. It was the way I immersed myself in guilt, allowing it to eat away at the reserves of energy and courage I'd previously had in abundance. All in all I hadn't done a very good job.

"Ok, now I do remember I set all these tests for myself, and I failed them pretty miserably." Aya had been waiting patiently, but there was obviously more to come.

"Maybe, maybe not, we'll come back to that later. But first how do you think all this relates to your backup plans?"

"I guess that whatever choices I and Sinead and Jocasta and maybe even others had made, there were always backups that would've led me down the same sort of overall path, so that I'd get to face the tests I'd planned to face."

"At *last!*" I sometimes thought the patronising routine went a bit far, but I also knew from experience that Aya needed to keep my feet firmly on the ground, so I just grinned back sheepishly as I responded.

"The trouble is we hear so much nonsense about karma on earth that it takes a while to sort things out again when we get back. I mean obviously now I can see that Sinead and I planned that she'd die young and I'd have to stay on in a wheelchair if I didn't pass the first test. But it can be really hard to see through all that talk of karmic punishment and debts and action and reaction and so on. All I knew was that it didn't resonate at all, but I still didn't get to the truth until now."

"Don't worry about that. There are plans afoot for all this to become a lot clearer for people on earth, the powers that be are working on it right now."

"Well that's good news, I guess I'll be able to take advantage of that next time." I thought for a moment, but something else was still troubling me. "I still can't recall what Sinead was supposed to get out of all this though. I mean, she did everything she could to help me wake up before the crash, and the crash itself certainly wasn't her fault, yet still she died young and had to leave our baby behind."

"Oh come on now, you know that not everyone hopes to *get* something for themselves every time. Sinead was completely unselfish when she planned that life with you. She knew most of the experiences were not primarily aimed at her, that she was mainly there to help you. She even accepted that if you messed up she'd have to die young."

"But that's incredible!" I was speechless again. I knew that Sinead was the most loving and giving soul I'd ever met, but the idea that she'd be *that* unselfish left me completely overwhelmed.

"No it's not, not really. After all, *you've* done exactly the same for *her* before now."

twenty three

It was something of a shock to be in Martha Bellows' shoes at first, but I soon got used to being a woman again as all the details of her life came flooding back. You see I *was* Martha. She was just another aspect of me, like Michael.

"There you go, you're not *so* bad after all. Maybe it's time to stop beating yourself up." I was back with sympathetic Aya again, although probably not for long.

"Well I guess if Sinead, as Saul, could fail these tests too, they *must* be pretty hard."

"Don't ask me, ask her."

In that instant Sinead joined us, looking more radiant than ever. We merged again and I felt my sense of inadequacy and failure melt away as she infused me with a knowledge that what we'd each been through as Saul and Michael was very, very hard. And we weren't only sharing love and reassurance, we were instantaneously sharing everything about both sets of lives so we could discuss them properly. Neither of us wanted to let go.

"When you two have quite finished." We separated but our hands remained intertwined.

"Good to see the old Aya's back again already, that didn't take long," I quipped, although she wasn't doing a very good job of hiding the fact that she too had been basking in the love we were radiating.

"Sorry teach, but it's been a while." Sinead's interjection was timely, she could always get round Aya much better than me.

"Forgiven, but come now, down to business. What can you tell me about all these lives and how they relate to each other?"

"It seems pretty obvious that we faced pretty much the same tests but with our roles reversed." Oops, I said that a little too confidently.

"Thank you Mister Smarty Pants, I'm very pleased to see you're finally getting to grips with everything and starting to feel at home again, but please keep your smugness under control." Fortunately Sinead was ready to ride to the rescue again, and I lost myself in the depths of her eyes as she gave us her take on it all.

"As I see it Saul's zealous adherence to dogmatic Christian doctrine was every bit as misplaced as Michael's more recent preoccupation with material wealth and all its trappings. Martha volunteered to help Saul maintain some balance, just as I did with Michael, but he too failed to listen first time round. His trigger for a second chance was the shock of seeing Martha hanged for sticking up for what was right while he did nothing about it, which is comparable to Michael's losing me and being crippled. With me so far?"

"Please carry on." Aya looked impressed.

"After that Saul *could've* been a powerful figure in rebuilding the shattered and traumatised community, and in introducing a more balanced spiritual message, just as Michael *could've* shared his experiences for the benefit of others. But instead we both allowed our guilt to stifle and consume us, although Michael slightly less than me – my degeneration as Saul was pretty extreme."

"Teacher's pet," I whispered. I just couldn't help myself, and I momentarily forgot that all this was telepathic anyway so Aya had picked it up.

"Well perhaps you can add to Sinead's wonderful appraisal by telling us what else *you've* learnt." Oh well. I always like to put myself under pressure.

"I think it's important that we understand our experiences weren't wasted at all, in fact quite the contrary. Nothing could've made it clearer to us what an unproductive and self-indulgent emotion guilt is, even if it sometimes comes across as chastening or humble. It was this misplaced, destructive reaction to the hugely testing circumstances we both faced in these lives that, more than anything else, prevented us from taking proper advantage of our second chance – and from being of some use to others."

It was a pretty eloquent riposte I felt, this time delivered with just the right amount of confidence but not arrogance, and designed to at least match Sinead's effort. Unfortunately, however, none of us could keep up the pretence of being deadly serious any longer, and we all collapsed into an energetic bundle of uncontrollable laughter. Eventually Aya managed to separate herself off and regain some semblance of control.

"Come on you two, we're nearly there, just get yourselves back together for a few moments more." We straightened ourselves out with some difficulty. "Now, tell me more about this guilt. Was it *at all* justified?" Again Sinead looked ready to take the lead.

"Given the culture in which Saul found himself, I guess his intransigence before and during the trial wasn't that surprising. And, once the mob turned on Martha and the two accused women, no one would've been able to intervene without being hanged along with them. Although I've got to admit that option seemed infinitely preferable to me afterwards as I lay on my bed wasting away."

"Very good Sinead, very good." Aya was looking sympathetic again, and even I didn't feel like making a joke. Sinead had made herself suffer so much at the end of that life as Saul, at least in part because of a love for me as Martha that had always gone pretty much unspoken. I directed a massive stream of healing love towards her, and she took it gladly. Then it was my turn again. They both looked at me expectantly.

"I suppose I have to accept what the police and everyone else said about the crash. Not even the best driver in the world, observing the speed limits and fully sober, could've avoided that truck. So forgiveness of others is important, but learning to forgive yourself is even more crucial. To cap it all off, it's wonderfully ironic that my insistence the crash was no *accident* was spot on – but for all the wrong reasons." Now *I* was on the receiving end of the most wonderful stream of healing love energy.

"You two can go off and relax as much as you like now. You deserve it."

twenty four

You can do pretty much anything you like here. *Anything*.

Where is *here?* It's everywhere and nowhere. It has infinite aspects on infinite planes, all with their own level of vibration and energy. At one end of the scale you've got ghosts still trapped on the earth plane with unfinished business, and their energies remain very heavy and slow. Then the planes get progressively faster and lighter until you get to those that we, and even Aya, couldn't get close to as yet.

One thing Sinead and I wanted to do was go back and experience Cancun together again – and we were able to recreate the whole place, beach and everything, just as it was when we were there. It wasn't the actual Cancun that any of you could fly to now. It was an energetic version. But to us, in the form that we're in, it felt exactly like being there again. We loved it.

Then we decided we'd have a bit of fun experimenting with what it's like to be different animals. We'd done this before but not for a while – in simple terms you just align yourself to the relevant vibration and away you go. Again you're not *actually* the animal itself, you're just tapping into the consciousness of that species. Sinead chose dolphins to start with – how original – but actually it was great fun. They're just as intelligent as many people have suggested, with a sophisticated communication system not far off being a proper language.

I thought I'd spice things up for us so I chose tyrannosaurs – yes, you can tap into extinct species as well, remember we're in what we call the *eternal now* – and boy what a contrast! They really weren't the sharpest tools in the box, but still the violent survival instinct was an interesting thing to experience. And the sheer, brute strength! Even Sinead found herself quite exhilarated when it was over.

About fifteen years in earth terms after I'd died, Jocasta came back to join us too. She wasn't that old, only around seventy, but she'd done everything she needed to, which was mainly making sure Zak grew up ok. So she just checked out when she was ready, in her sleep. We had a wonderful reunion, and the Old Man was especially pleased to see her since they share an extra special bond – even though they never met in that life – as Sinead and I do too.

You see we're all what you might call soul mates, or part of the same close soul group. I'm sure you've heard of this idea before. You know when you meet someone and you feel an instant, intuitive connection? Usually that means you have some sort of soul relationship stretching back into other lifetimes.

But different groupings have varying degrees of closeness, and we incarnate with all sorts. So don't be fooled into thinking we have a deep soul connection with all our partners and close family every time. My mother and the Old Man were not really soul mates at all, for example, and nor were Jocasta and her husband. And it's not the length of a relationship that matters so much as the quality and intensity of the interaction – which is why sometimes you remember a piece of advice, say from a complete stranger that you never meet again, but it stays with you for the rest of your life. Nor is it all sweetness and light with soul mates either, that's why Jocasta and I wound each other up so much in the early days. In fact only souls who are fairly close normally volunteer to trigger things that each of them needs to work on.

Zak's in our group too, along with the girl who'll end up being his wife, Zoe, and what a great team they're going to make! It's all planned don't forget, he's going to see her walking into a café and she's going to be wearing a massive straw hat, and in that instant he'll know he just has to follow her in and talk to her. And just in case he misses that trigger they've got several fallbacks, as usual. In any case we can still talk to both of them although they're on earth, especially when they're asleep. Aya does it even more than us, you might have guessed she looks after us all, and she has to keep prompting Zak and Zoe with dreams and intuitions and so on.

Perhaps I should take this chance to clarify what happened before, when I was Martha and Sinead was Saul. I bet you thought we'd be the other way around? Well the fact is that souls – I think it's about time we allowed ourselves to use that word in its proper context, don't you? – are essentially sexless. Now we all tend to prefer one sex or another when we incarnate, and for me it's being a man, for Sinead a woman. Yet we all swap over from time to time too, to gain different experiences and perspectives, and that's what the two of us did that time. It's this that sometimes leads to gender confusion and all sorts, and it's a real shame this doesn't get factored into that stale old nature-versus-nurture debate on earth.

We spend a lot of time here with our soul mates, relaxing or learning new things, and now the majority of us were properly together again Aya suggested we might like to go off and experience a completely different planet. This wasn't something we'd done before, and she thought it would be both fun and educational. As I tended to be the gobby one of the group, I took the lead.

"We've talked it over and we think it would be a fantastic idea."

"Where do you want to go then?"

"What are our options?"

"Couldn't you have guessed by now that they're pretty much infinite?"

"Yeah, that figures. We were thinking perhaps something that forms a real contrast to earth?"

"That won't be hard, earth is pretty unique in many ways."

"How so?"

"Why don't we discuss that when you get back? I think I've got just the place for your little holiday. By the way, you need to project yourselves again, you'll need to have a degree of energetic form for your trip."

"What's the weather going to be like then – shorts and flip-flops be ok?"

"Stop being childish and just decide what you want, I'm very busy and I've got other important things to do." For all that we liked to banter Aya wasn't normally *that* sharp with me, but she sounded deadly serious and I was quite taken aback – until she couldn't hold herself in any longer and cracked up. The others all followed suit.

"Ha bloody ha, very funny, why don't we make me the laughing stock, just for a change?"

"Honey, you do make it easy sometimes." As always Sinead was right.

"I suppose so." I tried to sound deflated and petulant but it was hard, I was excited at the prospect of the trip into the unknown. "Anyway, come on then, everyone choose what they're going to look like."

As I energetically adjusted my Native Indian loincloth I saw that Sinead had momentarily waited to pick up my thoughts so she could match me – or had she sneakily put the idea in my head first, she was so good I never did quite know. Anyway we now looked as we had when we'd shared a simple life together many centuries before, and it brought back wonderful memories. Then I turned to look at the other two.

"What the hell are you doing?" The Old Man was wearing a full NASA-style space suit, his huge helmet tucked under his arm.

"Well, no one said you had to be someone you've actually been, and I always fancied a go at this, they were just getting started when I left earth. And won't we need it anyway?"

"You really haven't got the hang of this, have you? We're not going to be *physically* present where we're going, just energetically." I was trying not to laugh, without much success.

"Actually you're going to a planet that's rather less physical than earth anyway, but still what you've said is right." Aya too was struggling to stop herself laughing. "Anyway the inhabitants won't be able to see you, so just look however you want."

"I'm staying like this then. Well, perhaps I'll leave the helmet behind." The Old Man's eyes were sparkling now, his face was the one I knew so well from the life just passed.

"You look lovely sweetie, just how I remember you," said Sinead as she admired Jocasta – who'd also chosen to project her most recent self, but had selected the most multi-coloured hippy outfit possible. Colours are much more intense and radiant here, and this was positively blinding!

"Oh no, not Jocasta Mark One," I groaned. I really wasn't sure I could take another dose of her.

"Stow it you, I've sorted all my karma and don't need to go back to earth like some people. I'll probably stay on this other planet as a fully enlightened master." We all cracked up again, until Aya brought us back to the job in hand.

"Why I ever agreed to work with you lot I really don't know. Anyway, is everyone ready?"

We all nodded.

There was a sudden energetic pull, a slight slowing of our vibrations and we found ourselves in the midst of the most beautiful scene imaginable.

The cloudless sky had a variety of hues from orange, through red to purple, and three pale moons were visible, silently watching over the planet. We were on a high plateau but the vegetation in the forest below was lush, thick and green, while off in the distance ice-capped mountains rose imperiously towards the sky.

We all just drank in the scene for some moments before Jocasta broke the silence, clearly impressed.

"This place is fab! It's like the Garden of Eden."

"Which never existed." I couldn't help it, but Sinead kicked me.

"Can't you switch that analytical brain off, just for once?"

dead man talking

"Sorry everyone." Time for a sheepish grin again. "Anyway, do you reckon this place is inhabited?" We all began to scan the broad expanse of valley below. There were few significant clearings in the forest, but I spotted a sizeable one off to our left. "Look, over there. If there's anyone around here, I reckon that's where they'll be." But it was a good few miles away so it was impossible to tell yet if there were any structures in it.

"Or any*thing.*" Sinead looked apprehensive. "This isn't one of those movies where the extraterrestrials have to be human with a silver suit on, or bits stuck to their faces."

"Ah but you forget, my sweet, whatever is or isn't here can't see us, so we're safe anyway."

"Just when I start to enjoy being with you again you always have to go and spoil it. No wonder Aya calls you Smarty Pants." Hands on hips, she stuck her tongue out at me.

"Come on then, let's get over there." The Old Man and Jocasta were already floating off hand in hand, looking hysterical in their contrasting outfits. With an exaggerated reluctance Sinead took mine and we followed suit.

We all swooped down low over the forest to get a closer look, and in one small clearing there was a herd of about fifteen grey-skinned animals. We slowed to look at them. Their heads, necks and torsos were horse-like but their legs were much thicker, almost like an elephant's. They moved slowly, some grazing on the low foliage at the edge.

"They're strangely beautiful. And so peaceful." Sinead was right up close to one of them now, a large female with several youngsters around her. She put her head up and sniffed the air, it was almost as if she sensed our other-

117

worldly presence.

"Can't be many predators around here though, doesn't look like they'd be able to run very quick." The Old Man was looking at the practicalities, as usual.

"Trust you. If you had your way you'd have a spear or an arrow or a gun aimed at them." Jocasta was clearly speaking from bitter experience.

"Not fair dearest! That's all in my past lives now. I didn't kill a thing in that last one, apart from a rabbit I ran over on my bike once, the bloody thing came out of nowhere and kept hopping from one side of my front wheel to the other until eventually it had me off. Put a big dent in the tank too, took me ages to sort it out."

"Thank *you*, but no one is very interested in your boring motor bike. Thank the Good Lord I decided I needed a break from you in that life." We were all laughing again now. By the way I don't want to put you off, not all soul groups are like this, but we find that laughter and mickey-taking work wonders. It stops us taking things, or each other, too seriously.

We sped up again and, as we approached the larger clearing, we moved up higher to get an aerial view.

"Well, there's your answer," I said. About twenty circular huts, made of wooden planks with some sort of thatch on the roofs, were arranged in a ring. In the middle a larger building looked like it had some sort of communal function. And that's where the inhabitants were, we could hear a low chanting coming from within.

"Come on, no time like the present, let's see what they're like." I dived down taking Sinead with me, the other two close behind. When we got to the large double doors they were shut, but after a quick hand-pass I realised our vibrations were high enough that we could slip straight through.

Inside were about fifty *people*. They looked exactly like humans, just shorter – their average height was probably about four feet – and they were all completely hairless. But their skin was tan-coloured and their heads and bodies were normal, so they weren't like the extraterrestrial greys we hear so much about. They were all naked so we could see their sex organs were human too, although the male members were rather larger for their size than we were used to.

"I'm not happy about that." I turned to the Old Man.

"Me either. Bloody liberty! Dearest, avert your gaze."

"Oh my sweet Jesus. We're right in the middle of a strange planet with a new race of people we've never seen before, and that's all you two care about?"

"I'm so glad we prefer being women, I couldn't stand having a brain that small." Sinead was cutting it a bit fine now, but as usual there was a general collapse until we pulled ourselves together.

Our hosts – not that they knew that's what they were – were obviously engaged in some sort of ceremony, and we watched, fascinated. At the front several of them were facing the others, they seemed to be the ones in charge, and every now and then they were chanting things that of course we didn't understand – it was just like being back in church really, Then they'd all start chanting together again, and swaying to the rhythm, as if they were in a kind of trance. Even we stayed silent for once, becoming quite transfixed ourselves.

When the ceremony broke up they all went back to their huts, so we floated in and out of several of them to see what was going on. The picture was the same wherever we went – there was complete peace and serenity throughout the community. They were all popping in and out of each other's homes, borrowing or lending, sharing food and so on. There were no raised voices, just complete calm.

"What a wonderful place!" said Jocasta, and Sinead nodded vigorously.

"Looks a bit boring to me," said the Old Man, but his dearest cut him short.

"Trust you to ruin the atmosphere."

"Seriously though, there's such a sense of simplicity and harmony." Sinead was spot on of course, and yet something wasn't sitting quite right with me. I just couldn't put my finger on it.

twenty five

We stayed on the planet for quite a while. Some of the time we split up and went off sightseeing as couples, other times we all stayed together. We came across a number of similar communities, and wherever we went the story was the same. Peace and harmony ruled. But in the end we'd had enough relaxation and decided to get back home.

"So what did you think?" Aya was waiting for us on our return, she seemed keen for a debrief.

"Not bad I suppose, at least it was relaxing." The Old Man was smiling, this was obviously supposed to represent high praise, but Jocasta wasn't having any of it.

"Oh come on, it was wonderful!" Sinead joined the chorus.

"Beautiful, absolutely beautiful."

"What about you?" Aya had turned towards me.

"Yeah, it was nice. But if I'm honest something wasn't quite right."

"What? You never said anything!" Sinead didn't look very happy to find there was something in my mind she hadn't managed to pick up on for once.

"Well, I couldn't work out what it was until the very end, so I cloaked it. And in any case I didn't want to ruin your holiday, you were having such a great time."

"Ok... thanks for that at least." She went quiet as I looked at her lovingly, so Jocasta chimed in again.

"Well I don't see any problem, I liked it so much I'd be happy to stay there. Is that what earth will be like one day, when we've gone back to a proper balance with our environment? They were all vegetarians, there was no hunting... idyllic." Aya was silent, but again she was looking at me.

"I don't think so somehow. You see there was something really, really important missing."

"Are you sure about that old son?" said the Old Man. "They looked happy enough to me."

"Look, I'm not criticising, I'm sure they were happy in their own way. But, as a group, we of *all* people know what the best expression of that is." They continued to just looking at me blankly. "Did you hear a single person *laugh?*"

"My God, no! You're right!" This time Sinead wasn't messing about. "How could the rest of us have missed that?"

"Well, like I said I didn't pick it up until the end, they all seemed to be having such a lovely, peaceful life, I guess it was easy not to notice."

"So what do you deduce from that, Mr Holmes?" Aya was obviously keen for me to delve deeper into the significance of all this.

"No one there seemed to express any real emotions at all, positive or negative. They just *were.*"

"And is that a good thing?"

"I think the Old Man was close to it when he said it was a bit boring."

"So how would you compare that to life on earth?"

"Well, of course it's bloody hard, we all know that, and there's lots of things wrong – anger and violence and disrespect and damaging the planet and so on, all of which were absent where we've just been. But boring it isn't, at least not most of the time. That's why they call it the *rich tapestry* of life."

"Exactly!" Aya seemed genuinely pleased, as if this time she couldn't even be bothered to bring me down a peg or two. The others were just listening intently. "So what do you think life on earth is really all about then?"

"Come on, I've done enough, someone else have a go." Sinead seemed to have switched on now and was more than ready to enter the fray.

"Of course! It's not about peace and harmony all the time. We can get plenty of that here, or in other places like that planet. It's about experience of the different extremes, the light and the dark, the good and the bad, the rough and the smooth."

"I believe to give it its proper name they call it *duality*," said Jocasta, whose light bulb had obviously just come on too.

"That's very good, all of you. But in simple terms it's experience of the different extremes of *what* exactly that really matters?" asked Aya.

"The full range of emotions." This time the Old Man had struck gold.

"Et voilà!" Aya was in her element again, beaming from ear to ear.

"And we can only do that on earth?" This question had been bubbling under ever since I worked out what was wrong on the planet, and now I was keen to get to the bottom of it. For once Aya didn't respond with one of her own.

"There are very, very few places that have the same level of duality, the same depth and intensity of emotions, as earth. It's a very hard proving ground, but it's also a great privilege to incarnate there. You grow and expand so much by facing the multiple emotional tests available." This was great stuff and we were all paying full attention.

"So can we just be clear about the real nature of the tests? All this sounds all very well, but what does it really mean *in practice?* I suppose there's some long, complicated set of rules." I hardly need tell you this was the Old Man with his practical head on, and again Aya was ready to answer herself.

"No, it's not complex at all, and you all already know the answer. There are only two kinds of emotion, *fear* and *love.* Every other emotion is a subset of one or the other. Anger, guilt, jealousy, revenge, shame, selfishness, all of these are fear-based, whereas empathy, sympathy, forgiveness, selflessness and so on are their counterparts on the love side. And however hard the situation you're facing, you should always be looking to turn fear into love. You'll always know which is the love reaction and which the fear one, because one will make you feel good inside and the other will feel uncomfortable. It really is as simple as that."

"So to the million dollar question. What are we all growing *for?*" This was Aya's opening gambit as we all sat around some time after our holiday escapade, and this time Jocasta opened the bidding.

"Well, isn't everything supposed to be just an illusion, especially what we experience on earth? Aren't we all meant to learn to see through it so that we're no longer tied to the karmic wheel, or whatever they like to call it down there?" We were all looking at her somewhat blankly, so she carried on.

"You know, if you work through all your karma and learn not to create any more you become an ascended master and don't have to go back any more, all that stuff." I wasn't happy with that at all.

"Look, it's fair enough to say that the physical world is a bit of an illusion because really everything is only energy. But to say that you have to learn to see through the illusion of *earthly life* – or even that what we're experiencing *here in the light* is just an illusion to be seen through too, because ultimately we're all One – surely that's going way too far? If all that was true there'd be no point to any of it – life on earth, reviewing and planning things here – and especially no point in going through all the trials we go through to gain experience and grow."

"I guess you're right." Jocasta seemed in no mood to dig her heels in on this one. "I suppose that 's just another one of those red herrings people on earth love to bang on about to sound clever, even when they don't really understand what they're saying at all."

"Like when some people bang on about karma." As usual I couldn't resist, which earned me a disapproving stare from Sinead. "Sorry Jocasta, you were fantastic after the accident, that was out of order."

"It's ok, I didn't take it personally. Anyway, what about this idea that we're all One. Is this where we need to bring Source into the equation? I was always hearing about people wanting to *rejoin* Source back on earth."

"Sorry, but I'm not sure about that one either," said Sinead. "I agree ultimately we're all One, but surely the level of vibration of Source is a long, long way beyond any of us who still have anything to do with earth?" Aya nodded but said nothing, so I picked up the thread.

"So we all aim to experience everything earth can offer us in terms of growth opportunities, and some tests take some of us longer to pass than others, but that's all fine because it's not a race and we all get there in the end..."

"I'm not sure he understood it wasn't a race last time," Sinead interjected, smiling at the others.

"Very funny! If I may be allowed to continue, even when we've done all that and no longer need to return, I suspect that's not the beginning of the end?" Aya nodded again and waited for me to finish the thought. "In fact it's just the *end* of the *beginning*." I felt very pleased with that one, and Aya allowed me to bask for a change before throwing the debate open again.

"So what exactly is our relationship to Source then?" There was silence for some time, before the Old Man put his analytical hat on.

"Well, I certainly don't hold with the idea that there's some sort of all powerful being somewhere who controls all our fates. I mean we know that's wrong because, apart from the fact he or she wasn't here when we arrived, we know we plan our *own* lives, even if we get a little help," he nodded towards Aya, "and we have free will to make our *own* decisions once we're incarnate too. On top of that Source is just energy, and we all came from that energy, so to some extent it seems to me that we must all *be* Source."

"Excellent." As usual though, Aya wanted us to take the idea further. "So are we individual souls, or are we just Source, which is it?"

"Oh Aya, Aya, Aya, you know that *nothing* is black and white around here." I gave her an extra big smile to make up for my lack of ability to resist the obvious jibe. "The

126

answer must surely be that we're neither one nor the other, but *both*, all at the same time." The others were looking as if that made sense, but the Old Man was particularly impressed.

"Oh, *that* I like!" He thought for a moment. "You know that's just like a hologram. I remember reading a bit about them before I left earth. The idea is that the part contains the whole but is definitely not the same, it's distinguishable from it." He had me really warmed up by now, because I'd come across it somewhere too and this was really resonating.

"You mean... how can we best put this? You mean we're all both individual aspects of Source, and full holographic representations of it, all at the same time?"

"Exactly that!" He was getting excited too, and I was on a roll now.

"And Source wants to experience anything and everything it can, that's why it differentiates into all the billions of aspects of itself that exist throughout the universe."

"And we're just a tiny part of that, gaining experience in our own little way on earth!"

"Hallelujah! We've cracked it!" The Old Man and I were jubilant, but the other three just stared at us.

"Men," they all said in unison.

Finally it got towards the time when I was ready to come back, and Aya was keen to give me a thorough briefing.

"There are some really important things I don't want you to forget when you go back this time. Call them a blueprint for life on earth, or a crib sheet, or whatever you like. As usual you know all of them already, but it's so important that you try to remember them once you're back in a physical body again, especially this time round."

She handed me a small scroll, and we merged and hugged and shared all our love for the final time for a while.

When she'd gone I opened it carefully and started memorising her pearls of wisdom.

PART THREE

twenty six

So, here I am again. Ready to enter the fray once more. It's been twenty-five years since I was last here, although of course to me it seems like only yesterday.

Some might say I'm a sucker for punishment but I'm not so sure. Those changes to the ground rules Aya was talking about have been put into effect – indeed giving me the scroll was part of that. Apparently lots of us were reporting back that it's been getting harder and harder to remember what we're supposed to be doing in the modern world, and not to get sidetracked by nonsense – whether it be about karma or illusions or just getting preoccupied with material things or whatever.

That's why the powers-that-be decided a while ago that lots of us coming back would be allowed to remember more. More about our real home in the light, more about our plans and why we're here, more about how it all works, more about what's really important. We'll still have some amnesia, because if we didn't not only would we be terribly homesick, but it would be like taking an exam when you've already got all the answers too. Our opportunities to grow by making mistakes would be too limited. Nevertheless I'm assured things will be quite a lot easier than they were.

Of course I'm not overly looking forward to being born, because I know that emerging from the comfort and cushion of the womb into the physical world proper is always a harsh and traumatic experience compared to our still-fresh memories of home. All those physical restrictions to get used to again, the heaviness and the slowness, everything weighing you down. That's why you've got it all wrong – death is infinitely superior to

dead man talking

birth!

As for my life plan, I've agreed to be involved in some sort of scientific research this time, although I'm not sure of the details. Does that sound strange for someone whose main lesson is still going to involve retaining their spiritual perspective while on earth? It might do, but it shouldn't. For some time now scientists have been pushing back their boundaries into metaphysics and so on. They're actually at the forefront of proving that the physical world represents a very limited set of perceptions that only scratch the surface of the full, multidimensional universe in all its glory. And that consciousness itself is multi-faceted, holographic, all-pervasive and all-connected. There you go, I need to practice my big words if I'm going to do this kind of work.

I've been told that the big plan, the real test for humanity as a whole, is for us to learn to do a far better job of balancing our technological progress with our innate spiritual wisdom. In the twentieth century the former went forward at amazing pace and left the latter behind. Now they have to come together again. That's what I, and many others like me, will be trying to work towards. Back home we're aware that a great many things are changing on earth, with old political and economic structures becoming more and more unstable, and young people using new forms of worldwide communication to cry, "Enough! We're not putting up with this any more." Underneath all this is a spiritual impetus, even though it's often unspoken, and apparently it ties in with huge changes to the earth's entire energy system.

Don't get me wrong, I've been warned this isn't going to be a bed of roses for those of us trying to spread a more spiritual message, whether from within the scientific community or in other ways. We'll still face the intransigence and even ridicule of those who have a vested interest in protecting the materialistic status quo – those who simply cannot conceive of any other way of living or thinking. We'll still have to have the faith and courage to do what we think is right, even when this is unpopular or controversial or misunderstood, and sometimes leaves us isolated. And we'll still have to have the patience to wade through the agonising periods of failure and self-doubt that will undoubtedly frustrate us while we wait for real progress to occur.

Only time will tell if we can, as the collective soul of humanity on earth, pull all this off. But then, as you now know, there's plenty of time. As much as is needed, in fact.

Before I go I must tell you about my new father. He's going to help me a great deal, especially with developing in the way I need to in order to fulfil my plan. I chose him especially for the job, and we planned this together, although coming from the previous generation I don't know how much of that he's going to remember himself.

In any case he's wealthy, having inherited a great deal of money from his father and used it wisely. He's intelligent and well-educated too, in fact already a well-respected physicist himself at the age of only thirty.

Perhaps you've heard of him? His name is Zak... Zak Prior.

Aya's Scroll

First, please remember that you really do control everything about your life. You planned all the major aspects in advance, so don't waste your time blaming chance or a fickle God or bad luck or whatever. Take responsibility, for everything. And when bad things happen, see them as opportunities to grow. Use your soul rather than human perspective and try to work out what the test is – after all, you set it for yourself – then try to pass it. And give thanks for your life, even more during the bad times than the good.

Second, don't waste your energy on negativity. Most of the time even when you're in physical form your thoughts and intentions still create the reality you experience – it's just that here the process is instantaneous, whereas down there it takes a while for things to manifest. So think positive. But also accept that sometimes you may be blocked from getting exactly what you want precisely because human life is supposed to include difficult tests. When that happens don't push against a locked door, just wait for the time to be right when it will open of its own accord. This is the meaning of the word surrender, and sometimes you'll need to do just that.

Third, work on your inner balance and contentment. Everything outside of you, even down to your beloved partner and children if you have them, has the potential to be taken away. Everything is ultimately impermanent, so love as much as you like, but don't get so attached to anything or anyone that you couldn't do without it or them. One day you may have to. Loving yourself goes right along with this. Always make regular time to do things that make you feel good, whatever they might be. Accept your faults, even if you're prepared to work on them, and never lose sight of your good points. There will be many, whoever you are.

Finally, balance coming from your heart and your head. Sometimes it's important to think something through logically, but if a decision is becoming a real struggle just stop and listen to your heart. It will know what to do. Above all, if you do nothing else, please remember my simplest of all messages. Choose love over fear every time. If ever you hear yourself worrying or being negative or angry or scared or jealous or whatever, just stop. Switch it right round.

Do the love thing. You know it makes sense ;-)

Aya xx

a note from the author

This book was originally drafted in 2005. The published version has been heavily reworked, but it still owes a great deal to the original creative input of Liz Swanson.

My sincere thanks also go to Pam Rosling for the title idea, and to all the wonderful reviewers whose input has proved invaluable: Mark Chatterton, Mark Goodman, Chris Hanson, Ken Huggins, Pam Lawton, Sue Liburd, Katherine Membery, Pam R again, Duncan Bain Smith and Andy Tomlinson.

None of the supposedly paranormal events depicted are based on mere imagination or conjecture. All of them have a foundation in the real experiences of a great many ordinary people, especially of the time between lives dramatised in Part Two. Meanwhile Michael's telepathic communication with his son during his NDE, via which a medical diagnosis is made, mirrors the true case of George Rodonaia.

If you're interested in finding out more about the evidence and concepts presented, full details can be found in *The Big Book of the Soul* and summaries in *The Little Book of the Soul*. There are also short film clips on YouTube, with links from my website.

Finally the advice in Aya's scroll is based on the detail in the pocket book *Your Holographic Soul, and how to make it work for you*. I hope you find it useful – if so a printable version is available on my website to stick on your wall.

Ian Lawton
November 2011

books by other authors

Note this is not a full or up-to-date list, it merely provides details of the books referenced by Michael in the early 80s. For a fuller bibliography see *The Big Book of the Soul*.

NEAR-DEATH EXPERIENCES

Moody, Raymond, *Life After Life*, 1975.

Sabom, Michael, *Recollections of Death*, 1981.

Ring, Kenneth, *Life At Death*, 1980.

REINCARNATION EVIDENCE

Ramster, Peter, *The Truth about Reincarnation*, 1980 (see also 'The Reincarnation Experiments' documentary produced by Ramster in 1983 at www.ianlawton.com/rsvideos.htm).

Iverson, Jeffrey, *More Lives Than One? The Evidence of the Remarkable Bloxham Tapes*, 1976 (see also 'The Bloxham Tapes' documentary produced by Iverson in the same year).

Stevenson, Ian, *Twenty Cases Suggestive of Reincarnation* (2nd Ed), 1974.

REGRESSION THERAPY

Cannon, Alexander, *The Power Within*, 1950.

Grant, Joan and Kelsey, Denys, *Many Lifetimes*, 1967.

Netherton, Morris and Shiffrin, Nancy, *Past Lives Therapy*, 1978.

Fiore, Edith, *You Have Been Here Before*, 1978.

other novels by the author

all published by Rational Spirituality Press *www.rspress.org*

AUTOBIOGRAPHY OF AN ANGEL (2012)
a novel about our hidden history and divine destiny

Our oldest traditions from around the world talk of gods and sages who introduced culture and civilization to our distant ancestors. In the modern world they are sometimes portrayed as visiting spacemen, or as survivors from the fabled lands of Lemuria and Atlantis.

Yet what if they were just highly experienced souls incarnating on earth with a job to do: 'angels' in physical form? What if many of them have been working away here, often unnoticed, for tens of thousands of years?

And what if, as we build up to perhaps the most climactic period in the whole of human history, one of them is finally prepared to reveal all? About how he taught our earliest forebears to bury their dead; about how he invented a way for our civilised, trading ancestors to estimate longitude at sea; about how he replanted the seeds of civilisation after the flood; and about our very destiny as the human race.

pocket books by the author

all published by Rational Spirituality Press *www.rspress.org*

THE LITTLE BOOK OF THE SOUL (2007)

true stories that could change your life

'This is a wonderful collection of stories, which I very much enjoyed. I will keep a copy for myself and happily pass the others on.' Peter Fenwick, fellow of the Royal College of psychiatrists and author of *The Truth in the Light*

'This is a very nice collection of intriguing cases. I hope it gets a lot of attention.' Jim Tucker, University of Virginia Division of Perceptual Studies and author of *Life Before Life*

'I like this little book a lot. It's a perfect hand-out for past-life clients, or especially skeptical friends.' Thelma Freedman, Secretary of the International Board for Regression Therapy

How did a Russian scientist left for dead in a mortuary for three days make contact with his neighbor's sick baby... and wake up with a cure that all the doctors had missed?

What about the Indian girl with memories of a past life... who astonished her former husband by reminding him how he had taken money from her just before she died?

Or the Australian woman who recalled past-life details of a carving on the stone floor of a small cottage... and was able to locate it under decades of chicken droppings when brought to England for the first time?

These amazing reports are not new age mumbo jumbo. They have been properly investigated by professional scientists. And they will make you think long and hard about who you are and what you are doing here.

YOUR HOLOGRAPHIC SOUL (2010)

and how to make it work for you

'I predict that the author's proposal of a holographic model of the soul will be one of the most important concepts of our time.' Hans TenDam, pioneering regression therapist and author of *Exploring Reincarnation*

'The idea of the holographic soul brilliantly solves many spiritual conundrums.' Judy Hall, pioneering regression therapist and renowned spiritual author

If you're a newcomer to spirituality, would you like to know about the evidence that your soul consciousness will survive without your physical body, and that you have many lives? Would you like to understand why you reincarnate, and what that means for how to approach your everyday life? And would you like to learn about your true relationship to God?

Or if you're a more experienced spiritual seeker, would you like to unravel the enigma of being part of All That Is and yet also an individual soul? And would you like to understand the oft-misunderstood interplay between experience and illusion, and between conscious creation and active surrender?

It's only now that we can finally answer all these questions and more using a spiritual framework that is logical, coherent and philosophically elegant. One that unites a modern scientific discovery with ageless spiritual wisdom in a simple yet revolutionary new concept... that of the holographic soul.

THE FUTURE OF THE SOUL (2010)

2012 & the global shift in consciousness

with Janet Treloar, Hazel Newton & Tracey Robins

So much has been written about 2012 and the global shift in consciousness. From catastrophic doom and gloom to sugar-coated messages that avoid the stark realities of what might lie ahead. But what if we were to be given channeled messages that are incredibly positive and exciting, yet also grounded? Well now we have.

These messages come from a diverse group of souls who refer to themselves as 'the council'. They provide information rarely if ever encountered elsewhere, including:

Everything is just as planned, even including over-population and the exploitation of earth's resources.

A similar shift occurred 26,000 years ago, but this time the conditions are deliberately very different.

So many souls are on earth now to take advantage of an incredible opportunity that has been known about, planned for and eagerly awaited for thousands of years.

The attention of the entire universe is excitedly trained on our planet. If you want to know why each and every one of us has a crucial role to play in this amazing transformation, as we blossom into our full spiritual potential, read on...

[*The Little Book of the Soul*, *Your Holographic Soul* and *The Future of the Soul* are also available in a large format compilation entitled *An Introduction to the Soul*.]

research books by the author

all published by Rational Spirituality Press *www.rspress.org*

THE BIG BOOK OF THE SOUL (2008)
Rational Spirituality for the twenty-first century

'I predict that the author's proposal of a holographic model of the soul will be one of the most important concepts of our time.' Hans TenDam, pioneering regression therapist and author of *Exploring Reincarnation*

'This fine book is masterly and scholarly.' Edith Fiore, pioneering regression therapist and author of *You Have Been Here Before*

Rational spirituality... surely this is a contradiction in terms?
How can spirituality be rational, when it relies on faith and revelation?
The simple answer is it does not have to any more...

There is persuasive evidence from near-death and out-of-body experiences that the physical brain is merely the instrument through which our soul consciousness expresses itself in the physical world. There is equally persuasive evidence from children who remember past lives, and from past-life and interlife regression, that we are individual souls who reincarnate to experience and grow.

A careful analysis of skeptics' arguments in each of these areas of research proves in most cases just how reductionist, and in fact illogical, they are. Nevertheless not all the evidence put forward by believers stands up, and careful discrimination is required. Such a balanced and in-depth critique of both sides of the argument is rare if not unique. Equally unique is the accompanying collation and comparison of the interlife regression research of a number of pioneering psychologists.

But what of the idea that 'we are all One', which is the universal message of all transcendental experiences? Can it be squared with the idea of the individual, reincarnating soul, or is this merely an 'illusion' in itself? Perhaps the answer lies in a theory of total elegance and simplicity... that of the holographic soul.

THE HISTORY OF THE SOUL (2010)

fallen angels, forgotten ancestors and karmic catastrophes

Was our planet once populated by a lost civilization that was destroyed? A fundamental reappraisal of the most revered ancient texts and traditions from around the globe, coupled with archaeological and geological evidence, suggests that it was. But what were our antediluvian ancestors like? Rather than huddling in caves to escape the ice age, were they expert navigators and astronomers who traveled far and wide? And did they have access to incredible technology, or was their culture defined far more by its spirituality?

Indeed, what was it that caused the massive surge in culture that began around 75,000 years ago and led directly to the evolution of the modern human race? What ongoing impetus allowed it to snowball so rapidly, compared to the slow but steady evolution of our hominid forebears over millions of years? Were divine sages really sent to introduce civilization to humanity, and if so how can we understand who or what they really were? Some sort of gods, or extraterrestrial visitors? Or were they just highly experienced souls incarnating on earth with a job to do, as they still do?

Is there evidence that our forgotten ancestors were almost completely wiped out? If so, how did this happen, and when? And was it just a random natural catastrophe, or was there an underlying 'karmic dynamic' related to their increasing preoccupation with the material at the expense of the spiritual? Most important of all, did their destruction have anything to do with universal energetic cycles? And, if so, what can we learn about the future we now face in the modern era? Are we once again surfing the crest of a huge energetic wave?

The veiled pointers to our hidden past have finally been unmasked as more than just the psychological constructs of philosophically primitive cultures. History is repeating itself. But what will happen this time round? And is the script already written... or can our actions now still help to dictate the outcome?

THE WISDOM OF THE SOUL (2007)

profound insights from the life between lives

with Andy Tomlinson

'This fine book provides much-needed information about everything from trapped spirits to demonic beings; from the purpose of incarnation to extraterrestrial realms; and from legends of Atlantis to global warming and humanity's future. I cannot recommend it highly enough.' Edith Fiore, pioneering regression therapist and author of *You Have Been Here Before*

'The research in this book poses questions that have rarely, if ever, been asked before.' Hans TenDam, pioneering regression therapist and author of *Exploring Reincarnation*

For thousands of years our view of the afterlife has been handed down to us by a variety of prophets and gurus

But in the last few decades thousands of ordinary people have been taken back into their 'life between lives' in the light realms

Their consistent reports form one of the most profound sources of spiritual wisdom ever available to humanity

And now two researchers have decided to push this source to its limits...

It is important enough that we should understand what happens to us between lives in the light realms: how we receive energy healing to lighten our vibrations; how we review our lives without judgment from higher beings; and how we choose and plan our next lives along with close soul mates, in order to face the lessons and experiences that will most allow us to grow.

But what if we could use the interlife experience to answer a host of more universal questions of spiritual, historical and philosophical importance? About everything from unusual soul behavior and soul development, through humanity's past and future, to the true nature of reality and time? What if multiple regression subjects came up with consistent answers? And what if they displayed wisdom so profound as to be way beyond any normal human capacity?

IAN LAWTON was born in 1959. Formerly an accountant, sales exec, business and IT consultant and avid bike and car racer, in his mid-thirties he changed

tack completely to become a writer-researcher specialising in ancient history and, more recently, spiritual philosophy.

In his non-fiction *Books of the Soul* series (see previous pages) he has developed the ideas of Rational Spirituality and of the holographic soul, and established himself as one of the world's leading authorities on the interlife. Short film clips discussing all these concepts can be found at *www.ianlawton.com* and on YouTube.

Ian is also a practicing current, past and between life regression therapist. This is his first novel.

Lightning Source UK Ltd.
Milton Keynes UK
UKOW021225161211

183917UK00009B/11/P